Chelsea and the
Outrageous Phone Bill

Best Friends

#1

Chelsea and the Outrageous Phone Bill

Hilda Stahl

CROSSWAY BOOKS • WHEATON, ILLINOIS
A DIVISION OF GOOD NEWS PUBLISHERS

Dedicated to two men of God
Lane Dennis
and
Jan Dennis
Thanks for believing in me!

Chelsea and the Outrageous Phone Bill.

Copyright © 1992 by Word Spinners, Inc.

Published by Crossway Books, a division of
Good News Publishers, 1300 Crescent Street, Wheaton, Illinois 60187.

Cover illustration: Paul Casale

First printing, 1992

Printed in the United States of America

Library of Congress Cataloging-in-Publication Data
Stahl, Hilda.
    Chelsea and the outrageous phone bill / Hilda Stahl.
        p.   cm. — (Best friends : #1)
    Summary: Angry with her father for moving their family to another
state, eleven-year-old Chelsea disobeys him by making long distance
calls to her best friend back home, but having Jesus in her life helps
improve the situation.
    [1. Moving, Household—Fiction. 2. Friendship—Fiction.
3. Christian Life—Fiction.] I. Title. II. Series: Stahl, Hilda. Best
friends : #1.
PZ7.S78244Ch 1991   [Fic]—dc20   91-33078
ISBN 0-89107-657-3

00   99   98
15   14   13   12   11   10   9

Contents

1

The Terrible News

Her blue eyes wide in shock, Chelsea held her breath as Dad stood in the middle of the kitchen and told them the worst possible news in the entire world. She glanced at her brothers across the table from her. Rob was struggling hard not to cry. He was twelve, a year older than she, and he hated to let anyone see him cry. Mike was eight, and the news hadn't bothered him in the least. Chelsea sagged back in the kitchen chair and stared at Mom and Dad. Mom had a tight smile on her face, and Chelsea knew she didn't like the news either, but was trying her best to put on a brave front. Dad looked ready to explode with excitement. Couldn't he see how all of them were feeling? Or maybe he was only looking at Mike, who also looked ready to explode with excitement.

"I know it's sudden," said Dad, slipping his arm around Mom's slender waist. Her red hair looked bright against Dad's gray suit. He stroked his nicely trimmed brown mustache. "But that's how Benson Electronics works. They want me as vice president." He rolled the words around on his tongue and said them two more times. "I've been aiming at being VP since I started working with Benson fourteen years ago."

"But we have to move away from here," said Chelsea just above a hoarse whisper. She'd lived in the same house all of her life. So had Rob and Mike.

"Living in Michigan will be different from Oklahoma," said Mom as she gripped Dad's hand. "But it'll be an adventure."

Just then the phone rang, and Mom almost jumped out of her skin. "I'll get it in the study," she said.

"I'll go with you," said Dad. They hurried out while the phone on the wall beside the refrigerator rang and rang.

Chelsea locked her fingers together and closed her eyes. She knew Mom hated leaving as much as she and Rob did. Mom and Rob were a lot alike— they both had trouble making friends. Mom would hate leaving the Sunday school class she taught and leaving Esther George, the friend she'd had since college.

Abruptly the phone stopped ringing. Outdoors a car horn honked. Chelsea heard the thud of her heart in her ears. She twisted a long strand of red hair around and around her finger.

"I'm gonna like living in Michigan where it snows all the time," said Mike as he jumped up from the kitchen chair. "Snowball fights! Snow forts! Sledding down long hills! Just like on TV." He did a flip right in the middle of the kitchen floor. He was great in gymnastics, and he took every opportunity to show off.

Chelsea frowned at him, but he didn't mind a bit.

"It does not snow all the time," said Rob. He was smarter than most people, and he wanted details right even when his world was crumbling around him. "But it does snow more there than it does here in Oklahoma."

"Who cares about snow!" Chelsea cried, jumping up and almost tipping over the kitchen chair. She pressed her hands to her aching heart. The big blue-and-yellow button that read *I'm A Best Friend* felt smooth against her hand. The neck of her yellow pullover felt tight against her throat. "What about best friends?"

"You can find friends everywhere," said Mike, doing another flip.

"You can't find friends anywhere," said Rob with a break in his voice. He was too shy to make friends.

Chelsea thumped her chest beside her *Best*

Friend button. "I have a best friend! And I won't leave her no matter what Mom and Dad say!"

Rob propped his bony elbows on the table and rested his chin in his hands. His wide blue eyes looked sad. "You have to obey, Chel. We all do."

Mike stood on his hands with his back arched just right and quoted, "'Children obey your parents in the Lord. For this is right!'"

Tears streaming down her freckled cheeks, Chelsea ran out the back door and through her yard into Sidney's yard. "Sid!" Chelsea called.

Sidney burst out her back door and met Chelsea under the huge cottonwood tree. "What in the world is wrong, Chel?"

Chelsea couldn't speak for a moment and just gripped Sidney's thin arms. She saw the concern in Sidney's brown eyes. Finally she said, "You won't believe what happened! It's the worst thing ever!"

"What?" asked Sidney, looking frightened.

Chelsea wiped tears off her cheeks and took a deep shuddering breath. "Sid, Dad just told us we have to move! To Michigan!"

"No!" Sidney shook her head, flipping her light brown hair around her shoulders. "But it gets too cold there. And people talk funny."

Chelsea nodded. "I know. But the very worst thing is I have to leave *you*. What will happen to our Best Friends Club? We just got it started and now I have to move almost a thousand miles away!"

Sidney's dark eyes filled with tears. "You can stay here with me! Don't move with your family."

Chelsea's heart leaped, then plunged to her feet. She rubbed her hands down her jeans. "My parents wouldn't let me."

"And mine wouldn't let me move to Michigan with you," said Sid sadly.

Chelsea sank to the grass and leaned back against the rough bark of the tree. This yard was as familiar to her as her own. They'd climbed the tree together, had mowed the lawn together, and had even kept Sidney's sister from eating sand from the sandbox when she was little. Chelsea pulled her knees against her chest and sighed. She and Sid had been best friends since before kindergarten. "I promise to write every single day! And I'll call as often as my folks will let me."

"Me too, Chel." Sidney knelt beside Chelsea. "We can be Best Friends Pen Pals!"

"It's just not the same," whispered Chelsea as she brushed tears off her cheek, then pushed her long red hair over her thin shoulders. She looked quickly around to make sure Sidney's brother Larry wasn't around. He always teased her about everything. She didn't see him, but she leaned close to Sidney anyway and whispered, "How can I survive without seeing Paul Ellison every day? He actually said hi to me at the mall last Saturday!"

"Oh, Chel! I never thought about Paul. That is

so sad!" Sidney's dark eyes glistened with tears as she caught Chelsea's hand and gripped it. "Maybe your folks will change their minds about moving."

Chelsea shook her head. "Dad is the vice president in the main office in Grand Rapids. Mom gave her notice today. We have to move in just two weeks!"

"But school won't even be out for the summer!"

"Mom is getting permission from our teachers for us to take early tests and be let out early."

"Why didn't they tell you sooner?"

"It was sudden, Dad said. He only learned about it this morning. And it's a *promotion* for him! He's excited. Can you believe it?" Fresh tears welled up in Chelsea's eyes. "He didn't give a single solitary thought to any of the rest of us! My whole entire life is totally completely devastated!"

Just then Sid's brother ran out the back door. He was thirteen and proud of his height and weight. He stopped in front of Chelsea and Sidney and flexed his muscles. "Want to feel my biceps, Chel?"

"No, Larry," said Chelsea.

"Get out of here, nerd face!" snapped Sidney.

"I wasn't talking to you, Dumbo," said Larry, making a face at Sidney. He always called her that because of the size of her ears.

"Don't fight, you two," said Chelsea. She'd been saying the same thing for the last five years—

ever since they started hating each other. She didn't understand how they could be so angry and so hateful. She and Rob were almost best friends—as close to being best friends as a brother and sister could get. But it was different with Sid and Larry. They hated each other like bitter enemies.

"It's all his fault that we fight," said Sid, scowling at Larry.

He made a face at her, then turned to Chelsea. "How come you've been crying?"

"It's none of your business, nerd face!" Sidney yelled.

"My dad got transferred to Grand Rapids, and we have to move in two weeks."

"Sorrowful." Larry always said that when he heard bad news. Then he laughed. "This is my chance to get rid of Dumbo here. I'll pack her in the moving van. When Mom and Dad ask about her, I'll say she was kidnapped by some Far Eastern dudes."

Sidney rubbed her hair down over her ears and stuck her tongue out at Larry.

Chelsea sighed heavily. She couldn't make them stop fighting no matter how hard she tried. "I'll talk to you later, Sid. I have to start packing. Mom said I have to check through all my stuff to see what I want to take. If I leave it up to her, she'd throw it away." But Chelsea didn't move.

"When will you leave?" asked Sidney.

"The middle Saturday of May."

"Then we'll spend every single minute together."

Chelsea nodded. "Every minute!"

"I'm going to throw up," said Larry. He ran around the house to get away from them.

Chelsea touched her *I'm A Best Friend* button as she looked at Sidney. "I promise to be your best friend as long as I live."

2

The Ravines

Chelsea wanted to close her eyes tight and not look around her as Dad said, "Here's our new neighborhood. It's a subdivision called The Ravines."

"I see some boys my age!" cried Mike with his nose pressed against the back window of the station wagon. "But I don't see any snow."

"I heard they had snow the end of April, but it melted quickly," said Dad, chuckling.

Chelsea looked at the houses they passed. She hated them! They didn't look like the rambling one-story house she'd lived in all her life. The houses were two-story with dormers on the second floor and decks off the backs. The houses looked like identical twins dressed differently to keep from looking alike. But it didn't work. They still looked alike. Dad pulled up to the two-car garage at a gray house with white shutters.

"We're home," Dad said proudly.

Chelsea studied the wide front yard. Yellow daffodils bloomed in a spot surrounded with big rocks. The houses on either side were farther away than Sidney's house had been from theirs. All the yards had large trees. They were almost bare—not leafed out like back home. A house across the street had a giant rock with numbers painted white on it. The house numbers on their house were tall brass numbers. She glanced at Rob. He was staring down at his hands, fighting to keep from crying. Mike scrambled out the back door and ran across the grass like a wild person. He did flips all the way back to the car.

"We'd better go inside," said Mom, trying to sound cheerful.

"The furniture should be in place," said Dad. "I marked which furniture went in which room, and the men said they'd take care of it."

Chelsea bit her lip as she slowly stepped out of the station wagon. A cool breeze blew, and she shivered even though she wore a sweater and jeans. She hoped the moving men had kept her special box safe. It held her Best Friend Club information, along with a photo of Sidney.

Just then Chelsea glanced at Mom and saw tears in her eyes. She was chewing on her bottom lip the way she did to keep from bursting into tears in front of anyone. Anger at Dad rose in Chelsea. She glared at him, but he didn't notice. He was striding toward the white front door to unlock it. Rob was still sitting in the station wagon.

"Come see the new house," said Dad with a happy laugh. "We're the first folks to ever live here. You'll all like it a lot." He motioned to them. He'd flown here to find the right house, then had bought it on the spot. "Come on."

Chelsea slowly followed Mom while Mike ran eagerly to Dad. Rob caught up with Chelsea and walked with her. His auburn hair looked as if he'd rubbed his fingers through it. His denim jacket was zipped to his chin.

"I hope my computer's ready to use," Rob said with a catch in his voice.

"It probably will be," said Chelsea. She knew he wanted to bury himself in a computer game so he wouldn't have to think about living in a strange place.

Dad opened the front door with a flourish. "Welcome home, all you wonderful McCreas!"

Mike ran inside, and Mom slowly followed with Chelsea and Rob right behind her. Dad stepped in behind them and beamed with pride.

"What do you think?" Dad asked happily.

Chelsea looked at the wide front hall with a closet on one side and a plant on the other. One arched doorway led to the living room and another to a hallway with an open stairway and a few doors further on. The house was much bigger than home had been. The walls were soft colors that went well with the furniture. "I'm going to look upstairs," said Chelsea, suddenly feeling anxious to check on her special box.

Dad caught her arm. "No. We're going to look at it together as a family. We want to enjoy it together."

Chelsea wanted to jerk away from Dad, but she knew he'd scold her. She waited until he stepped away from her, then she rubbed the feel of his hand off her arm. She couldn't ever remember being this angry at him. Once when he wouldn't let her spend the night with Sidney she'd been angry, but she'd gotten over it almost immediately. She would *never* get over this anger.

She reluctantly followed the family into the living room, the dining room, the kitchen, Dad's study, and even into the laundry room. The washer and dryer looked brand-new, but Chelsea knew they weren't by the nick on the side of the dryer where she'd dropped the softball bat.

"We'll go to the basement before we go upstairs," Dad said, looking very mysterious. Today he wore a blue pullover sweater and jeans instead of a suit. He looked more like a big brother than a dad. "I have a special surprise to show you."

Chelsea bit back a sigh, and she noticed Mom and Rob did too. Mike raced down the carpeted steps after Dad.

"It's a rec room," said Dad proudly as he flung his arms wide.

Chelsea gasped in shock as she looked around. There was a pool table, a Ping-Pong table, a game table with a shelf behind it loaded with board games, a dart board on the wall, and a large TV with Nintendo and a VCR.

"This is quite a surprise," said Mom hesitantly as she pushed her hands into the pockets of her jeans.

"I get to play Mario on Nintendo!" cried Mike, dropping to the floor in front of the TV.

"Not now," said Dad.

Rob looked helplessly at Chelsea. She knew he was thinking how terrible it would be to be stuck down here instead of in his room with his computer. Chelsea wondered who'd ever come play with them since they didn't know anyone at all. Mike would probably have several friends before the day was up and fill the rec room with noise. She didn't want to make friends, and Rob didn't know how.

"Now look over here," said Dad with a wide pleased grin. He opened a trifold door, and behind it was a snack bar with a refrigerator. "Isn't it great? I hope you all like my surprise."

"We do!" cried Mike, doing handsprings back and forth across the carpeted floor.

Mom said, "It's nice, Glenn."

"I thought you'd like it, Billie. You once were the Ping-Pong champ."

"That was a long time ago," she said weakly.

"It's like riding a bike," said Dad, laughing as he hugged Mom tight. "You never forget. We'll have friends over, and you can show off your skill."

"I don't know," said Mom, sounding close to tears.

Chelsea wished this very room had been in their real home. Sidney would've loved it. Maybe even Paul Ellison would've come to visit.

"Now for the upstairs," said Dad, leading the way, taking two steps at a time.

Mike raced up after him.

Mom patted Chelsea and Rob. "This is a very nice house. We'll learn to like it here. You'll see."

Chelsea swallowed the lump in her throat and slowly walked up the stairs. A few minutes later she followed the family from the master bedroom to Mike's, then to hers. Sunlight shone through the two windows onto the blue-and-mauve bedspread she'd had for a year now. Her furniture looked strange in the room because there was more floor space than in her other bedroom. Suddenly she noticed a white phone on her desk. Her eyes lit up. She could call Sidney whenever she wanted in the privacy of her own room! It wasn't as good as being with her, but it was better than nothing. The minute she could get away from the others she'd call Sidney and see what she was doing.

In Rob's room Chelsea stood in the doorway and looked around. Everything was the same, yet something was different—something more than just a larger room.

"Where's my computer?" asked Rob in a strangled voice as he touched his desk. He also had a phone, but he didn't seem pleased about it. He was only concerned about his computer.

Dad cleared his throat. "Your mother and I decided to give you a summer without your computer."

"What?" cried Rob, his eyes wide and his face ashen. He clenched and unclenched his fists at his sides.

"You need to get out around people," said Mom firmly. "You don't want to be my age and still afraid of meeting new people."

"I don't care about people!" cried Rob. "I just want my computer!"

Chelsea wanted to comfort Rob, but she didn't know what to say. If she had a computer, she'd give it to him. She frowned at Dad. She knew it was all his idea. How else would he ruin their lives?

"I've spoken to the woman at the corner grocery store about you working for her," said Dad.

Rob sank to his bed, helplessly shaking his head.

"You'd sweep and dust and stock shelves," said Mom, stepping closer to Dad.

"I don't want the job!" cried Rob.

Chelsea gasped in surprise. Rob had never raised his voice in anger. Mike did that a lot, and so did she, but never Rob. He was really upset. Couldn't Dad just give Rob the computer and let him be happy again?

Dad sat beside Rob and slipped an arm around him. "Rob, you're a wonderful boy and a good son. I love you. I want you to be the very best person you can be. Hiding behind your computer is harmful to you. You need to have a little push to get you among other folks. We're giving you that little push."

Rob jumped up, his fists knotted. "I won't do it! I mean it!"

"Rob!" Dad rose to his feet and towered over Rob. "You will obey. And you will not shout at me or your mother. Now calm down and control yourself. Later you will go to the store to meet Mrs. Lemmy and to learn the hours you'll work. You will also take a turn mowing the lawn. The lawns here often have to be mowed twice a week."

Chelsea shook her head and gritted her teeth. Dad had better not mess her life up more than he already had!

Dad turned to Chelsea almost as if he'd read her mind. "While I'm assigning jobs, Chelsea, I might as well tell you what we expect of you."

Chelsea groaned.

"You'll be in charge of Mike while your mother and I are gone," said Dad.

"No!" cried Mike, shaking his head hard. "I'm eight, and I don't need a baby-sitter!"

"Oh yes you do, young man," said Mom sternly.

Mike clamped his mouth shut, but his eyes flashed with anger.

Chelsea shrugged. "I watched him at home lots of time. I can do it here."

"And you did a fine job with him," said Dad. "Your mom is going to get a part-time job, so that'll leave you here with Mike part of each day." Dad turned to Mike. "There's a park nearby. And there's plenty of room in the yard to play. You can't spend more than an hour a day in front of the TV."

Mike shrugged.

Chelsea frowned. Mike had always watched TV or practiced his gymnastics, leaving her free to read or talk with Sidney. Now it would be different.

"Let's look around outdoors," said Dad. "I want to show you everything!"

Chelsea bit back a groan. She was tired of this together thing. At home Dad had been too busy to do things with them except on Sundays. It had been better that way.

Reluctantly Chelsea walked around the yard with the family. The wind seemed to bite through her sweater and jeans. How could it be so cold so late in May? Even the freckles all over her felt cold.

Dad walked to Chelsea and tugged a strand of her red hair. "I saw a girl your age next door. You can go see her now and get acquainted. She just might end up being your very best friend."

Chelsea covered her *I'm A Best Friend* button with her hand and clamped her jaw tight. No one but Sidney Boyer was going to be her best friend!

"You kids walk around and check your new home out on your own," said Dad as he caught Mom's hand in his. "We're going inside for a cup of coffee."

Rob looked longingly toward the house, but he didn't move.

Shouting, Mike ran around and around the yard.

Chelsea slowly walked toward the big bush that separated their yard from the neighbors. She might as well meet the neighbor girl, then forget her. They'd never be best friends no matter how nice she was!

3

Roxie Shoulders

Chelsea stopped at the edge of her yard and looked back at Rob. His head was down and his shoulders bent. She felt sorry for him. "Want to come with me?" she called.

He hesitated, then ran to her side. "I hope nobody's home," he said.

"I'm not going to like the girl anyway," said Chelsea with a toss of her head. "I don't care what Dad says!"

Rob stuck his hands in his jacket pockets and hunched his thin shoulders. "Dad shouldn't keep my computer from me. It makes me so mad!"

"I know."

"He's mean."

Slowly Chelsea walked into the yard next door. She was glad Rob was with her even if he wouldn't do any of the talking.

Just then a girl ran out of the house, slamming

the door behind her. She had short dark hair and wide brown eyes. She was tall and slender and wore a bright orange-and-green sweatshirt and green pants. She stopped short when she saw Chelsea and Rob. "Hi," she said without smiling. "Who are you?"

"I'm Chelsea McCrea, and this is my brother Rob. We just moved in next door."

"You talk funny."

"No, I don't," said Chelsea, suddenly angry. "You do!"

The girl laughed. "Where are you from anyway?"

"Benson, Oklahoma," said Rob, surprising Chelsea.

"I'm Roxann Shoulders, but everybody calls me Roxie. And don't bother teasing me about my last name. I'm tired of all the jokes." She looked past Chelsea and Rob. "Oh no!" She ran across the yard toward a small brown dog. "Get out of here, Gracie! You're not going to dig in the flower bed this time!"

Chelsea watched in horror as Roxie picked up a switch and swung it at the dog. "Don't hurt that dog!" cried Chelsea as she ran toward Roxie to stop her.

Roxie struck the dog on its back leg. It yelped and ran away.

Chelsea caught Roxie's arm and yanked the

switch from her and flung it to the ground. "How can you hurt that little dog?"

Roxie put her doubled fists on her waist and glared at Chelsea. "How dare you tell me what to do! That dog keeps digging up our flower bed, and nothing will grow. Mom wants to win the Prettiest Flowers Contest this year. And she can't if that dog keeps ruining it!"

"Why don't you put up an electronic dog guard?" asked Rob.

Chelsea stared at him with her mouth hanging open.

"What's a dog guard?" asked Roxie, turning to Rob with interest. She was the same height as Rob and almost as thin.

"It's an electronic line you bury in the ground," said Rob. He explained how it worked as if he weren't shy at all.

Chelsea suddenly felt angry at Rob, but she didn't know why. That alarmed her, and she forced the feeling away. She would not start hating Rob like Sid hated Larry!

Slowly Chelsea backed away. She waited for Rob to follow, but he and Roxie kept talking. Finally Chelsea walked out of the yard and back into her own. She looked across the street at the house with the large rock. The house was white with black shutters. A girl with straight black hair walked around the house into the front yard and stopped beside the rock. Chelsea could tell by the color of her skin and hair and the high cheekbones that she was a Native American. In Oklahoma she'd gone to school with several Cherokee, two Iowas, and a few Shawnee. She remembered when everyone had called them Indians, then changed to calling them Native Americans because it sounded better.

The girl waved to Chelsea, then ran across the street toward her. "Hi. I'm Hannah. What's your name?"

"Chelsea. We just moved in."

"I know. I watched when the moving van came two days ago, and I saw all of you get out of your station wagon a while ago. Your little brother does great flips. I wanted to come sooner, but Mom needed me. She's going to have a baby soon, and she can't be on her feet long."

Chelsea liked Hannah. "Mike's the baby in our family. I was three when he was born. Mom's getting a part-time job, so I have to watch Mike part of the time."

"I have three sisters. Lena's nine. Vivian and Sherry are twins, and they're eight."

"I have a twelve-year-old brother, Robert. We call him Rob." Chelsea glanced toward Roxie's house. He was still there! "I just met Roxie. Do you know her?"

"Yes." Hannah sighed heavily. "She doesn't like me much."

"How come?"

"Because I'm Native American. She's prejudiced."

"That's too bad."

Hannah shrugged. "I'm used to it."

"Just like I'm used to being teased about my red hair and freckles." Chelsea rubbed her hands up and down her arms. "I used to try to wish my freckles away, but it didn't do any good. My best friend never teased me about them though."

"Who's your best friend?"

"Sidney Boyer," said Chelsea with a catch in her voice. She told Hannah all about Sid and the fun they'd had together and their Best Friends Club.

"I've never had a best friend," said Hannah enviously. "Could we be best friends?"

Chelsea shook her head. "I promised Sid she'd always be my best friend."

Hannah sighed heavily. "I wish I knew how to get a best friend."

"We made a list that tells how to make friends. Would you like to read it?"

"Yes!" Hannah looked over her shoulder at her house. "But I can't right now. Mom might need me. I guess I'd better go see."

Chelsea didn't want Hannah to leave, but she didn't say anything. She knew how important it was to obey. "We can talk later maybe," said Chelsea.

Hannah nodded and smiled. "I hope you can

teach me how to make friends. I'll come over again as soon as I can."

"Okay." Chelsea smiled happily. She was glad she'd met Hannah. She watched until Hannah ran inside her house, then turned and walked slowly to her door. Rob was still at Roxie's!

In her bedroom Chelsea opened her special box and took out Sidney's picture. Tears blurred Chelsea's vision, and she pressed the picture to her heart. How she wanted to talk to Sid!

"I will!" whispered Chelsea, quickly drying her eyes. She dropped to her chair and picked up the white phone. Sidney answered on the second ring.

"Hi, Sid."

"Chel!" cried Sidney with a squeal.

"I miss you so much! What are you doing right now? What did you do since I left?"

"Yesterday I went to Sunday school and church, of course. I saw Paul Ellison, and he said hello to me."

"No! Tell me every single detail!" Chelsea carried the phone to her bed and sank to the floor beside it. She listened to Sidney, savoring every word.

After they'd talked several minutes Chelsea told Sidney about the rec room. "I wish you were here right now—we'd play darts. You're still the champ, Sid."

"I want a rec room just like yours!" cried

Sidney. "Do you have any idea how much fun we'd have?"

Later Sidney said, "There was a new girl in Sunday school yesterday . . . Megan Richfield. She's nice. She has a brother as mean as mine. And she's in fifth grade. I saw her today and ate lunch with her at school."

Jealousy ripped through Chelsea, and she couldn't speak for a while. Finally she said, "Remember we promised we'd stay best friends forever."

"I would never forget that! Megan is nice and we hang out together, but that doesn't mean we're best friends."

Chelsea sighed in relief. She told Sidney about Roxie and about Hannah. "I like Hannah, but we will never be best friends, even though she'd like to be. She's never had a best friend . . . Or even a friend. I'm going to show her the list we made up on how to make friends."

"I thought that was *our* list," said Sidney harshly.

Chelsea hesitated and finally nodded. "You're right. If I show her the list, that could lead to more and I might start liking her too much. I won't show it to her. I'll tell her I changed my mind."

"Good."

They talked several minutes longer, then hung up. Chelsea smiled happily as she propped Sid's picture up against the white phone. She looked over the list of "How to Make Friends." It would help Hannah a lot to read the list, but she'd agreed not to show it to her. Chelsea's heart sank a little. How could she tell Hannah that she wouldn't help her learn to make friends? Chelsea pushed the question aside. She wouldn't think about Hannah. She'd find Rob and see what he was doing. Maybe he'd want to play Ping-Pong since he didn't have a computer.

Chelsea found Rob alone in the kitchen eating an apple.

Rob asked her, "How come you left Roxie's?"

"I won't talk to a girl who hits dogs," said Chelsea, lifting her chin high.

"She said she won't do it again," said Rob.

"Oh sure!" Chelsea sat across the round table from Rob. "I can't believe you talked to her."

Rob flushed. "I was surprised too. I had to tell her how to keep the dog away."

"Well, I don't like her at all!"

Rob shrugged. "*I* do."

"That's a big surprise." He usually didn't like anyone.

"I told her about my job with Mrs. Lemmy. She said she's nice. She said she'd walk to the store with me except her mom wanted her to help watch her little sister."

"I'll go see Mrs. Lemmy with you."

Rob bit his lip, then nodded. "I guess I better

go before I get too scared again. Roxie told me where the store is."

A few minutes later they stopped outside the brick store. It had a wide picture window, two heavy glass doors, and a small parking area in front. A gray Nissan was the only car parked there.

Rob trembled and stepped back from the door. "I can't go in," he whispered hoarsely.

"Sure you can. Come on." Chelsea led the way, and finally Rob followed. A bell tinkled over the door. A woman looked up from the cash register which sat on a cluttered counter to the left of the door. The place had the combined smells of cat food and a butcher shop. "We're looking for Mrs. Lemmy," said Chelsea.

"That's me," said the woman with a laugh. She was about Mom's age and short and plump. Her blonde hair was curled all over her head, and her blue eyes sparkled. "What can I do for you?"

Chelsea looked at Rob, and he finally stepped forward.

"I'm Rob McCrea," he said with a break in his voice. "My dad talked to you about me working here."

"He sure did!" Mrs. Lemmy rubbed her hands over the stains on her white apron. "I liked the way he talked. What a cute accent!"

Rob flushed.

Chelsea got ready to grab Rob if he started to run away.

"When can you start?" asked Mrs. Lemmy.

"When do you want me?" asked Rob.

Chelsea bit back a shocked cry.

"Any time," said Mrs. Lemmy.

Rob swallowed hard. "I guess tomorrow."

"Your dad said you won't be going to school, so how about coming in the morning about 9?"

"I'll be here."

Mrs. Lemmy told him what she'd pay, and Chelsea suddenly wished she could work there also.

Outside the store she caught Rob's arm and said, "You're so lucky!"

He brushed her hand off, his face red. "I'm not going to work there! I mean it!"

"But you said you would."

"Well, I won't! I don't know how to stock shelves or sweep the floors or anything!"

"Mrs. Lemmy will show you how."

Rob shook his head. "I can't come to work. What if I can't do the work? She'll think I'm stupid."

Chelsea stamped her foot. "Rob, you're being stupid right now! Mrs. Lemmy is nice. She won't expect you to know everything. Let her show you how to do the work, then do it. You're smart enough to catch on to any kind of work."

"Do you really think so, Chel?"

"Of course!"

Rob sighed. "I guess I can try."

"You sure can!" Chelsea slapped Rob on the back. "You're able to do a lot more than you think. I bet you'll be the best worker Mrs. Lemmy ever had."

"I hope so." Suddenly Rob smiled. "And I did make a friend today . . . Roxie Shoulders."

Chelsea bit her lip to keep from telling Rob he'd chosen a horrible person as a friend. She'd never be friends with Roxie—not in a million years.

Chelsea's stomach cramped with hunger, and she glanced at her watch. It was time to help make dinner. "I'll race you home for dinner."

4

Hannah and Kathy

Chelsea waited until Mom left for a job interview, then ran to her bedroom and called Sidney. Mike was taking his hour on Nintendo, so she knew she had free time for her best friend.

"Sid, you can't believe it, but Rob actually has a job!" Chelsea told about Dad taking away Rob's computer and about Mrs. Lemmy and the money Rob was making. "Rob worked all morning for Mrs. Lemmy, and now he's mowing the lawn. He even talked to this really mean girl next door. Roxie's her name. You wouldn't like her a bit. Larry might since he's mean too."

Sidney talked about her new friend Megan. "We ate together again today, and after dinner she's coming over to work on a special social studies assignment with me. She's almost as smart as you, Chel. Only she's right-handed, not left-handed like you."

Chelsea didn't like Sidney comparing her with Megan, but didn't say anything.

Just then the doorbell rang. Chelsea frowned. "I have to answer the door. Mike's in the rec room, so he'll never get it. I'll call you again soon."

"Bye, Chel. You're still my very best friend. Did you remember to find a special Scripture for us today?"

"I didn't, but I will." They usually shared a special verse from the Bible every day, but Chelsea had forgotten ever since Dad had told them the terrible news about moving.

Chelsea quickly hung up and ran downstairs to the front door. Hannah stood there still dressed in her school clothes.

"Hi, Chelsea. Mom said I could visit for a few minutes."

"I'm sorry, but Mom doesn't let me have company when I'm watching Mike." Chelsea's stomach knotted. She knew Mom wouldn't mind Hannah stopping in if she didn't stay long, but . . .

"Could I just read your 'How to Make Friends' list?" begged Hannah.

"I'm sorry, but you can't. Maybe another time." Chelsea saw the pain in Hannah's eyes and almost gave in, then remembered her promise to Sidney.

Hannah slowly walked away, her head down and her steps slow. A car drove slowly past on the street. The small dog Gracie stopped on the sidewalk and barked.

Chelsea closed the door and leaned weakly against it. She had never been mean to anyone in her life before. How could she be so mean now? "I'll call Sid back and tell her I want to give Hannah the list."

Upstairs in her bedroom Chelsea waited for Sidney to come to the phone. When she did she was laughing and out of breath. "What took so long?" asked Chelsea sharply.

"Megan was telling me this great joke," said Sidney. "It was so funny even Larry laughed."

Chelsea's throat tightened. She didn't like Sid laughing at Megan's jokes.

"Why did you call back?" asked Sidney.

"I want to give Hannah, the girl I told you about, the paper on making friends."

"Sure . . . Okay . . . Go ahead, Chel. You didn't need to call about that. Talk to you later." Sidney hung up before Chelsea was ready.

Tears filled Chelsea's eyes as she stared at the phone in her hand. Finally she hung it up, wiped her tears, and pulled the list for Hannah from her special box. The tin box had once held Oreo cookies, and when it became empty she'd asked Mom if she could keep it for her special things. The *r* was almost rubbed off the word *Oreo*, and she'd written her name in bold black marker across the middle of the tin box. She pushed the lid on and ran downstairs with the paper clutched in her hand.

At the basement door she called, "Mike, come here. We're going to the neighbors for a while. You can meet two girls your age."

"In a minute, Chel. I have to win this game first."

Chelsea sighed heavily. "Come on, Mike! You can always play later."

"Promise?"

She closed her eyes and sighed heavily. "Yes! Now come on!"

Mike ran up the steps and pushed past Chelsea. "Well, come on, Chel! I don't have all day, you know."

She felt like punching him, but she didn't. What was wrong with her anyway? Lately she was mad at *everybody*.

"I get an extra half hour because you made me quit now," said Mike as they walked outdoors.

"All right, you big baby!"

"I am not a baby!" Mike's blue eyes flashed with anger. "You're the baby."

Chelsea bit back the sharp answer as she ran across the street with Mike beside her. She knocked on Hannah's door.

Hannah opened the door. Her eyes were red-rimmed as if she'd been crying. She didn't speak.

Somewhere behind her the TV was going. The smell of a freshly peeled orange hung in the air.

"I brought the paper to you," said Chelsea. "I'm sorry I didn't give it to you a while ago." She held it out, but Hannah shook her head and refused to take it. Chelsea dropped her hand as blood pounded in her ears. What was wrong with the Native American girl?

"It won't do any good to read it," Hannah said gruffly. "Nobody wants to be my friend."

Chelsea's eyes stung with tears. "I'm sorry," she whispered.

"Can we go now?" asked Mike, starting to walk away.

"No!" snapped Chelsea. She turned back to Hannah. "Could we meet your sisters?"

"They're busy," said Hannah.

"Maybe another time," said Chelsea weakly. She turned away and walked slowly down the sidewalk toward the street. She saw Rob park the lawn mower in the garage, then run into the house. The lawn looked neat, and she liked the smell of the freshly cut grass.

Mike dashed across the street, shouting to Chelsea that he was going right back to his game. "And I get an extra half hour!" he called over his shoulder.

Just as Chelsea reached her yard, Hannah

called to her. She reluctantly turned, ready to run to the house if Hannah said something mean to her.

Her long hair bouncing on her shoulders, Hannah raced to Chelsea's yard. "I'm sorry, Chelsea! I am so sorry! I do want to read your list! I do want to be friends with you even if we can't be best friends!"

Chelsea's heart leaped. With a glad laugh she held the paper out to Hannah. "If you have any questions, ask and I'll help you all I can."

Hannah looked at the list, then at Chelsea. "You have a Scripture here. Are you a Christian?"

"Yes! Are you?"

"Yes!"

"This is wonderful!" cried Chelsea. "Come in and let's talk." Mom had prayed for special Christian friends for all of them, but Chelsea hadn't been interested since she hadn't planned on having friends. But now she was excited about learning Hannah was a Christian too.

"I thought your mom didn't want anyone inside when she's gone."

"We can sit on the front steps," said Chelsea, flushing. When they sat down she said, "Mom really wouldn't care if you came inside for a while. I was upset when I said that. I'm sorry."

"I say things I shouldn't say when I'm upset too," said Hannah. She rubbed the paper over her

41

legs. "'To make friends you must be friendly,'" she read.

"That Bible verse is so true," said Chelsea. "To get to know someone you must ask about them . . . learn what interests them . . . talk about *them* instead of yourself." It was all on the list of "How to Make Friends." She and Sidney had made up the list after talking to their parents and their Sunday school teacher.

"What interests you, Chelsea?" asked Hannah.

Chelsea giggled. "I know what you're doing."

Hannah giggled too. "But I really want to know. Do you like to read?"

"Yes. And I'm left-handed."

"So is my dad!"

"No one is left-handed in my family but me."

"Do you like music?" asked Hannah.

"Yes. Do you?"

"Yes. I take piano lessons." Hannah wrinkled her nose. "Sometimes I hate practicing though."

Chelsea liked talking with Hannah. She wanted to talk longer, but Hannah had to get back home to help her mom.

Just as Hannah ran home Rob walked outdoors. He sat beside Chelsea with his chin in his hands.

"I can't live without my computer," he said.

"I can't live without Sid," she said.

They both sighed as Mike stepped out.

"Let's go to the park," he said.

"Might as well," said Chelsea, jumping up. "Want to come, Rob?" She couldn't remember when he'd gone to the park back home.

"Sure," he said much to her surprise.

At the park Mike ran to join some boys his age playing on the tire obstacle course. Rob walked to the wishing well and leaned against it, counting the coins in the clear water. Chelsea stood beside him and looked at the others in the park. There were teenagers playing tennis, a few girls swinging on the swings, and several kids sliding down the slide. She noticed a blonde-headed girl her age chasing a little girl dressed in a cute pink blouse and slacks.

The little girl dashed toward the wishing well. When she was almost to Chelsea, she tripped and fell flat, then burst into tears.

Chelsea scooped up the little girl and brushed dirt off her face and clothes. "You're all right," Chelsea said gently.

"Megan!" cried the blonde girl as she ran to her and bent down to look her over. "Are you all right?"

Megan nodded as she rubbed her fist across her nose.

Chelsea stepped away from Megan. She hated that name. It was the same name as Sidney's new friend.

The blonde girl smiled at Chelsea. "Thanks for helping Megan. My name is Kathy Aber. It's spelled

43

a-b-e-r but is pronounced a-bear. I have to tell everyone that or they say my name wrong."

Chelsea laughed. "My name is Chelsea McCrea. This is my brother Rob."

Rob flushed and mumbled hello, then walked away.

"He's shy," said Chelsea. "Well, he was shy back home in Oklahoma, but he's not as much here."

"Kathy, I want to swing," said Megan, tugging on Kathy's arm.

"All right," said Kathy.

"I'll go with you," said Chelsea, falling into step with Kathy while Megan ran on ahead.

"Did you just move here?" asked Kathy as she pushed Megan.

"Yes. Have you always lived here in Middle Lake?"

Kathy nodded and sighed. "I wish I could say I lived in some wonderful place like Wyoming or Colorado. I've always wanted to live on a ranch and have lots of horses. Do you know how to ride?"

"Not very well."

Kathy stepped back from the swing and let Megan glide. "I have never in my whole life ridden on a real horse! I've been on the carousel horses, but that's all."

Chelsea laughed. "I always get sick riding on it."

"I get sick riding the roller coaster!"

"I've never had the courage to ride one."

"I was scared, but I did it because my brother Duke dared me."

Chelsea suddenly realized she liked talking with Kathy. She felt as if she'd always known her. And she hadn't even said a word about Sidney, her very best friend. Guilt rose in Chelsea and she said quickly, "I have to get going."

"Where do you live?"

Chelsea hesitated, then told her.

Kathy said, "I live just outside The Ravines— on Kennedy Street! It's close enough for us to visit together. Want to come over later today after I finish watching Megan?"

Chelsea realized she wanted to very much, but she shook her head. It would be too easy to like Kathy too much and tell her all the secret things she'd told only Sidney. "I'm watching Mike. He's the blond boy walking on his hands over there."

"He's cute," said Kathy, laughing as she watched Mike go into his gymnastics routine. "He could be in the Olympics."

"He wants to be," said Chelsea. "But Mom and Dad don't want him to leave home to train."

Kathy lowered her voice. "Sometimes I wish Megan lived somewhere else. I get so tired of watching her all the time." Kathy gasped. "Please don't tell anyone. You're the very first person I've ever told that to."

Chelsea backed further away from Kathy. They didn't dare share secrets! She'd promised Sidney. "I have to go now. Bye, Kathy. Bye, Megan."

Chelsea raced away with Kathy and Megan shouting good-bye behind her.

5

The Phone Bill

Chelsea pressed the phone tighter to her ear and bit her lower lip to hold back a sob. Her bedroom suddenly felt closed in. Her unmade bed and pile of dirty clothes looked worse than they had before she'd called Sidney. The last few days that she'd talked to Sidney, Megan had always been there.

"I want you to talk to Megan, Chel," Sidney said as if it were the best idea in the world. "Please . . . For just a few minutes . . . I know you'll like her."

Chelsea gripped the phone so tight her knuckles turned white. She didn't want to talk to Megan! She wanted to tell Sid not to talk to or see Megan ever again in her life.

"Chel!" Megan said excitedly. "Sid has told me all about you! I feel as if I know you. How do you like living in Michigan? Is it freezing cold? Did you make any new friends yet?"

"It's alright here," said Chelsea stiffly. She

47

heard the whirr of the lawn mower. Rob was mowing the lawn again. The grass grew fast, especially after a rain. "I don't have new friends." She'd stayed away from Hannah and Kathy the past two weeks out of loyalty to Sidney. Why hadn't Sid stayed away from Megan out of loyalty to her?

"You should get out and make friends," said Megan cheerfully. "You'll like it better there if you do. I know I'd hate living here if it weren't for Sid. She's my very best friend."

Tears burned Chelsea's eyes, and she sagged against her desk as if she'd been stabbed in the heart. "I guess I'd better go."

"I bet your phone bill is really high from all the calls you've made," said Megan.

Chelsea gasped. The phone bill! She hadn't even thought about that. How high would it be? How much did it actually cost to talk an hour a day to Sid?

"I know how high mine was. And my dad made me pay for it myself. But my grandma helped me. She said she thought I'd learned my lesson, and she gave me fifty dollars to help pay it. I'm sure glad she did!" Megan talked on and on, but Chelsea stopped listening.

After a long time Sidney took the phone. "I gotta go now, Chel. It was nice talking to you. I'm glad you like Megan. We're getting ready to go swimming now."

Chelsea hung up and sat without moving a long time.

Two weeks later Chelsea frowned at the kitchen calendar beside the phone. It was almost the end of June. It seemed like the month they'd been in Middle Lake was ten years long. Every day had dragged. The only bright spot in each day had been the hour she'd talked to Sidney, but now even that wasn't a bright spot. Megan always talked to her too.

And Chelsea thought about the phone bill constantly. She thought about the phone bill every time she heard Mom and Dad talk about their expenses. She thought about the phone bill every time the phone rang. She even dreamed about the phone bill. She thought maybe she should tell her mom what she'd done. But she just couldn't bring herself to tell. Mom still didn't have a job. She'd worked two weeks to fill in while someone was on vacation, but then she'd gone back to having interviews or applying for work.

"I wish Esther was here so I could talk to her," Mom had said day before yesterday while they were eating dinner. "I talked to her on the phone a couple of times, but I couldn't stay on long because of the cost. And she's called me. I wish it didn't cost so much to call her!"

Chelsea had almost choked on the carrot she was eating.

"Billie, there are a lot of women at church," Dad had said. "Make friends with them. Out of all of them you could find another best friend."

Mom had turned pink and hadn't answered. Chelsea knew Mom didn't want a new best friend any more than she did.

She came back to the present and thumped the calender and turned to stare out the window above the kitchen sink. She saw Rob drive past on the lawn mower, looking happier than she'd seen him since they'd moved. He actually liked mowing the lawn! Mike had gone to the grocery store with Mom. She'd asked Chelsea if she wanted to go, but she'd said no. She wanted to wait for the mailman, but she didn't tell Mom that.

Just then she heard the special clink of the mailbox lid. She ran through the house to the front door just as the mailman walked away. She opened the door, and a gust of wind flipped her hair and brought in the smell of the freshly cut grass.

She pulled the stack of mail out of the small box and ran to the kitchen table with it. Her legs trembled as she sank to a chair. Quickly she looked through the pile. There was a letter from Grandma McCrea and a credit card bill. And the phone bill!

Chelsea's heart hammered so loud she was sure Rob could hear it outdoors, even over the roar of the lawn mower. She started to open the envelope, then stopped. Dad would wonder why she'd opened it.

Maybe she could hide it and he'd never know what she'd done. She shook her head. The phone company would send another bill next month. She was trapped!

Slowly she carried the stack of mail to Dad's study where they put the mail every day after it was sorted. She stuck the phone bill on the bottom of the pile. She trembled, and her mouth turned dry. She jerked the phone bill out and held it. Maybe she should keep it until she found the courage to tell Mom and Dad about her phone calls to Sid.

Chelsea trembled and almost dropped the envelope. "Jesus," she whispered, then stopped. She hadn't prayed since they'd moved here. The prayer stuck in her throat. Finally she gave up.

She'd tell Mom and Dad about the bill as soon as she found the courage. Just then she realized the phone bill wasn't her fault at all. It was Dad's fault! He'd forced her to move away from Sidney. It was his fault that she was so lonely she had to call Sidney. Chelsea narrowed her eyes and pressed her lips tightly together. "It *is* Dad's fault!" Now she could show them the bill.

"Chelsea, we're home!" called Mom.

Chelsea's heart zoomed to her feet. Quickly she stuffed the phone bill under the couch cushion, then ran to the kitchen. Could Mom tell by her face she was guilty about something? When Chelsea was younger, Mom could always tell.

"I brought chocolate chips home," said Mom as Mike waved the yellow-and-brown bag. "We'll make cookies."

"And I brought M & Ms, so we could add those too," said Mike as he pulled out the candy treats. "I get to help. Mom said."

Chelsea's stomach was in such a knot that chocolate-chip cookies didn't sound good at all.

"Did you get the mail already, Chel?" asked Mom as she set the gallon of milk in the refrigerator.

"Yes. It's in Dad's study." Chelsea turned away to hide her flushed face as she pushed the box of raisin bran into the cupboard. "Why?"

"Oh, I just wanted to see the phone bill."

Chelsea froze. "Why?" she asked, forcing her voice to stay calm.

"I hate to see how much it is," said Mom with a loud sigh. "We have to be very careful of our spending until our house in Oklahoma sells."

Chelsea sagged against the counter, her legs feeling like a hot marshmallow.

"That's why it's important for me to get a job," Mom said as she put away the spaghetti and sauce. "Once the house sells, I could even stay home full-time if I wanted."

Chelsea forced herself to continue helping put the groceries away while her mind whirled with ways to keep Mom from seeing the phone bill. She finally realized there was no way out. Dad's fault or not, she'd have to tell them what she'd done, then find a way to pay her share. She had almost sixty dollars in her bank to use later in the summer when they went to visit Grandma and Grandpa. Maybe her share wouldn't be more than sixty dollars. That thought cheered her enough that she could help mix the chocolate-chip cookies without bursting into tears.

After dinner while Rob and Mike were outdoors tossing the football around, Chelsea said with her head down, "Mom, Dad, I have to talk to you."

Dad looked up from the book he was reading. He'd said he wanted to cut back on TV watching so he could read more. So far he was doing it. "You sound serious," he said as he dropped his book on the small table beside his recliner.

Mom was writing a letter, and she looked up with her pen held high. "Did you break something?" she asked sharply.

Chelsea shook her head. Mom was talking about the time Chelsea had dropped and broke an antique sugar bowl that Mom treasured. It had taken three days to get up the courage to tell her about it. "I didn't break anything." Her voice cracked, and she sank weakly to the edge of the couch.

"Honey, don't be afraid to tell us," said Dad. "We love you."

Anger shot through Chelsea. How could Dad say he loved her after forcing her to leave Sidney?

"Just tell us, Chel. You're beginning to scare me," said Mom.

Chelsea jumped up and forced her trembling legs to support her. "Just wait here. I'll be right back." She ran to Dad's study and pulled the phone bill out from under the couch cushion. She groaned as she pressed it to her chest. How could she show the bill to them? She'd stopped wearing her *I'm A Best Friend* button last week. They wouldn't understand why she needed to talk to Sid so much. She took a deep breath, then ran back to the living room. "Here," she said, pushing the bill into Dad's hand.

"What's this?" he asked.

"I called Sidney, and it'll be on the bill," said Chelsea weakly. "I didn't think of the cost when I called." But she knew she'd continued to call even after Megan had mentioned the cost. Chelsea pushed that thought aside. "I'm sorry," she whispered.

"Oh my," said Mom, shaking her head.

Chelsea dropped to the edge of the couch and locked her icy hands in her lap as she watched Dad tear open the envelope.

He looked at the bill. His eyes widened, and his mustache twitched. He groaned, then whistled, then looked at Chelsea. "You did indeed call Sidney! Three hundred dollars' worth!"

Chelsea fell back, too weak to speak, too weak to even burst into tears.

"Part of it must be mine," said Mom, kneeling beside Dad's chair and reading the bill with him.

"Yours isn't very big," said Dad. "But Chelsea called during daytime hours when the rates are the highest."

Chelsea managed to sit back up. "I . . . I . . . will . . . pay my share."

"I know you will," said Dad sternly. "Do you have plans for making that kind of money?"

Chelsea shook her head. "But I'll find a way."

Mom sighed heavily. "Honey, I told you not to call Sid."

"I forgot."

Her mom gave her that knowing look.

"It's over and done with," said Dad. "Here's what I'll do. I'll pay the bill so we don't get our phone shut off, but you'll pay me back—every cent. We'll have to use our vacation money to do it. But by then our Oklahoma home should sell, and we'll be able to go on our vacation. If it doesn't sell . . ." He left the sentence dangling and spread his hands wide.

"I'm sorry," whispered Chelsea. "I didn't mean to do anything wrong. I will find a way to make money."

"Ask the Lord to help you," said Dad. "He loves you, honey. He wants to help you."

Chelsea nodded, but she knew she couldn't pray. She hadn't been able to for over a month.

Later she walked outdoors, hugging her sweater around her to keep from shivering in the evening air. Just how was she going to make money?

Just then Roxie stepped from behind a tree. "Hi, Chelsea. I was just coming to see you."

"Why?" They hadn't spoken in days.

"I wanted to ask if you'd do something for me." Roxie lifted her chin as if to dare Chelsea to refuse. "Rob said you might."

Chelsea almost turned away, but she stood with her hands in the pockets of her jeans and her head tilted. "What is it?"

"I need help with Mom's flowers." Roxie sounded close to tears.

"What's wrong with them?" Chelsea looked across her yard to Roxie's.

"Gracie got in them again! Some are tore right up, and others are knocked down. Mom will be home in an hour, and I have to fix the flowers before she gets here. Rob said you're good with plants."

Chelsea shrugged. "I guess I am." She *was* good with flowers. Everybody always said she had a green thumb. When she was little she thought her thumb would actually turn green, but it never did.

"Will you help me? Please?"

Chelsea nodded, surprising herself. It might help her forget her own troubles.

"You will?" asked Roxie in surprise.

"Sure. Why not?"

"Thank you!" Roxie clasped her hands under her chin, and her eyes glistened with tears. "Oh, thank you! Can you come right now?"

Chelsea shrugged. "I'll tell my mom and be right over."

"I'll wait for you." Roxie moved restlessly. "Just in case you change your mind."

"I won't."

A few minutes later Chelsea knelt beside Roxie and worked on the flowers. The ones that were broken off she trimmed with scissors she'd brought with her for that very reason. They reset the torn-up plants. Then Chelsea carefully watered all of them. By the time they were finished it was dark. Lights shone out from the windows, lighting paths across the lawn. For just a fleeting minute Chelsea felt good about her work. But the good feeling left as thoughts of her outrageous phone bill returned.

"Thanks for helping me, Chelsea," said Roxie.

"You're welcome." Chelsea suddenly realized she could charge Roxie for her help. She hesitated, then blurted out, "How much can you pay me?"

"Pay you?" cried Roxie, her eyes large in her thin face. "You didn't say anything about pay!"

"I need the money," said Chelsea coldly. "Do

57

you really think I'd help you for nothing when we're not even friends?" Chelsea wanted to grab back the ugly words the minute she'd spoken them, but couldn't. She thought about apologizing, but didn't.

Roxie knotted her fists at her sides. "Oh, all right, I'll pay you. I sure can't understand why Rob thinks you're so great. You're not!"

Chelsea's stomach knotted, but she lifted her chin and looked squarely into Roxie's eyes. "I think I'm worth five dollars."

A few minutes later Chelsea held the five-dollar bill in her hand. It burned her fingers and turned her heart to stone. Slowly she walked home, the dirty money in her hand.

6

Fights

Chelsea paced from one end of the rec room to the other while she tried to think of ways to make money. Mike was almost finished with his hour on Nintendo, then they were going to the park. How could she make money if she had to continue to watch Mike? It wasn't fair! Maybe she should tell Mom she wouldn't watch Mike anymore. Mom could hire a baby-sitter. Chelsea frowned and shook her head. That would mean her parents would have to spend more money, so that wouldn't work.

She stopped behind Mike and watched as he tried to win his game. She inched her foot forward, and just as Mike was ready to scale the last obstacle she bumped his arm, making him lose.

He whirled around and glared up at her. "Why'd you do that? Now I get another game."

"No way! You're stopping right now, Mike. We're going to the park. Shut off the TV and come on!" Anger burned inside Chelsea, and she couldn't understand it at all. What was wrong with her? She'd never done mean things to Mike, especially such a mean thing as to make him lose his game.

His face red with anger, Mike ran up the steps, shouting, "Mom! Mom, Chelsea kicked me and made me lose!"

Chelsea walked slowly after him. Soon he'd remember Mom wasn't home. She heard him burst into tears, and she knew he'd realized Mom was gone. She stopped in the kitchen and waited at the back door.

Mike hurried into the room. "I won't go to the park with you! I mean it, Chelsea McCrea!"

"You have to go. Dad said so." Chelsea's jaw tightened. "And you know Dad always gets his way."

Mike glared at Chelsea, then pushed past her and ran outdoors.

She followed him, walking slowly. She glanced toward the flowers in Roxie's yard. They looked fine. She tried to feel good about it, but couldn't. She still felt the burn of the five dollars in her hand. Even after she'd stuffed it in her bank, she'd felt it.

At the park Chelsea sat on a green bench and watched Mike stand alone by the slide. He looked ready to burst into tears again, but she knew he wouldn't for fear of other kids seeing him. He hated to be called a baby.

Kathy Aber walked into the park with her little sister Megan. They were dressed alike in pale green shorts and white T-shirts with green balloons appliqued on the front. Chelsea watched Kathy swing Megan. How would it feel to have a little sister? A lot better than a little brother!

After several minutes Megan ran to the sandbox to play with three girls her age. Kathy looked around and saw Chelsea.

"She'd better stay away from me today," muttered Chelsea.

But Kathy walked right up to Chelsea and stopped a few feet in front of her. Two light green barrettes held back her blonde curls. "Hi, Chelsea. You look so sad I had to come over and see if I could help you."

Tears filled Chelsea's eyes and she blinked hard, but they kept coming.

"You *are* sad!" Kathy dropped down beside Chelsea and slipped her arm around her. "Tell me what's wrong, and I'll help all I can."

Chelsea didn't want to tell Kathy anything, but the words poured out of her—about Sidney and Megan, about the phone calls, about her anger at Dad.

"I'm so sorry," said Kathy each time Chelsea took a breath.

"And now I have to pay Dad almost three hundred dollars!" wailed Chelsea as tears flowed down her freckled cheeks.

Kathy pulled a tissue from her pocket and pushed it into Chelsea's hand. "This was for Megan, but you need it worse. Now wipe your tears and blow your nose, then we'll talk about ways for you to make money."

Chelsea blew her nose and wiped off her cheeks and eyes. It felt good to have Kathy tell her what to do. "It'll take me forever to pay Dad back."

"No, it won't. Others find ways to make money. We will too."

Chelsea bit her lip and sighed. "Thank you for being nice to me."

"I like you," said Kathy smiling. "When we first met, it felt like we'd known each other forever."

Chelsea nodded and smiled. "I was afraid I'd tell you my secrets that I should tell only my very best friend." She hung her head. "I guess I was right."

"It's all right that you told me." Kathy pulled her legs up against her chest and wrapped her arms around her knees. "Now, we need a plan. What can you do?"

Chelsea frowned. "I can't do anything!"

"Of course you can! Think for a while."

Chelsea rubbed her hands down her jeans, then pushed back her red hair as she thought. "I baby-sit

Mike. I am good with flowers. I help with house-work and with mowing the lawn."

"That's wonderful! See? You can do a lot of things!" Kathy beamed with pride. "Now all you have to do is find someone who needs work done."

"I could ask people at church."

"That's right! And in the neighborhood."

Chelsea thought of Roxie, and she flushed. "I did something really bad to Roxie."

"What?"

Chelsea quickly told her. It seemed the most natural thing in the world to tell Kathy her thoughts and actions. "I know I should give the money back."

"Yes, you should," said Kathy, nodding hard.

"But how can I? Roxie is so . . . so . . . I don't know! Rob likes her, but I don't!"

Kathy leaned close and whispered, "I don't like her either." She sat back and grinned sheepishly. "I have never in my life said that to anyone!"

"I won't tell," said Chelsea. It felt good to share secrets again.

"I know we're to love Roxie because Jesus said to," said Kathy.

"I forgot." Chelsea squirmed uneasily.

Just then Megan started crying. "I'd better go see what's wrong," said Kathy with a loud sigh. She jumped up and ran to Megan.

Chelsea watched Kathy brush sand off Megan

and hug her close. It made Chelsea think of Mike and all the times she'd helped him feel better. She looked around for him. She couldn't see any blond boy wearing a red T-shirt and blue jeans. She jumped up, suddenly feeling frantic. Had Mike run off because he was angry at her? She dashed toward the wishing well and looked past it into the wooded area. She saw two girls, but no sign of Mike. She ran to the baseball field to see if Mike was watching the practice, but he wasn't among the kids there either. She saw a crowd of boys on the far side of the field and she ran toward them, her heart thudding painfully.

Boys crowding into a circle shouted louder as Chelsea reached them. She saw two boys scuffling on the ground. One of them was Mike!

"Mike!" she cried in alarm. He'd promised he wouldn't fight anymore. The last time he'd been in a fight he'd gotten a black eye and a gash on his cheek.

The boys parted, and Chelsea reached down for Mike. "Stop it, Mike!" Suddenly someone pushed her, and she sprawled to the ground beside Mike and the boy he was fighting with. She scrambled up, flushing with embarrassment. The boys laughed and whistled. She darted a look around, but couldn't tell who'd dared to push her down. She trembled as she turned back to Mike. "Get up, Mike!" She caught his arm and jerked him to his feet. One eye was swollen shut, and his nose was bloody. The other boy looked as bad.

"Let 'em fight!" cried a tall boy with short black hair. "Gavin almost had him whipped."

Mike flung up his head. "He did not!" Mike pulled away from Chelsea. "*I* almost had *him*!"

"You're not going to fight," said Chelsea sternly. She frowned at the tall boy. "Don't make more trouble!"

"Nick, don't let her push you around," said Gavin, looking up at the tall boy. They looked so much alike that Chelsea was sure they were brothers.

"She won't push me around," said Nick, stepping right up to Chelsea. "You and your brother better get out of here, Freckles."

Freckles! The terrible nickname sent her anger soaring. She lunged at Nick and, catching him off guard, sent him sprawling to the ground. The boys laughed and shouted.

Chelsea stared down at Nick, suddenly alarmed at what she'd done. "I'm sorry," she said in horror. "I am *so* sorry!"

"Let's get out of here, Chelsea," said Mike, tugging her arm.

"Chelsea, is it?" asked Nick as he slowly stood. He brushed off his jeans as he looked her up and down.

She nodded slightly, suddenly finding it hard to

breathe. "Chelsea McCrea from Oklahoma. This is my brother Mike."

"Let's go!" cried Mike, pulling harder on Chelsea.

"Come on," said one of the boys in the crowd. "The fun's over. Let's go." He led most of the others off across the field.

"I'm Nick Rand, and this is my brother Gavin," said Nick. "We live at The Ravines."

Chelsea's eyes widened. "So do we! At 2958 Ash."

"We're about three blocks away at 1540 Hornbeam." Nick smiled. "Maybe Gavin and I will see you two again."

Chelsea nodded. "We have a great rec room with lots of games." Why had she said that?

"Do you have Nintendo?" Gavin asked Mike.

"Yes." Mike listed the games he had with it.

"I'll be over later. And I'll beat you at every game," said Gavin with his blue eyes narrowed.

"No way!" Mike shook his head hard. "I'm too good."

Chelsea smiled at Nick, and he smiled back. "I hope I didn't hurt you."

"You didn't." Nick tugged on Gavin's wrist. "Let's go. Bye, Mike. Bye, Chelsea."

"Bye," Chelsea and Mike said together as Nick and Gavin ran away.

Chelsea stepped closer to Mike. "Let's get you

cleaned up before Mom sees you," she said as she looked after Nick until he reached the sidewalk. She tugged Mike's hand. "Let's go."

At home Mike ran to the bathroom to wash while Chelsea sat on the front steps with her chin in her hands. Would she really see Nick again? He was cute, even if he had called her Freckles.

Rob jerked open the front door and stepped out, his eyes flashing fire. "Just what do you think you're doing, Chelsea McCrea?"

She jumped up with a frown. Rob never yelled at her. "I'm just sitting here. What's wrong?"

"You know." Rob stepped right up to Chelsea. He was only a couple of inches taller, but he seemed five feet taller.

"Why are you mad at me?" asked Chelsea, trembling. "It wasn't my fault Mike got in a fight. He's not really hurt, even though his eye looks bad and his nose was bleeding."

"I'm not talking about Mike. It's Roxie Shoulders!"

Chelsea frowned, then bit her bottom lip. "Oh."

"How could you charge for helping with her flowers? She would've been in big trouble if her mom had seen the flowers. I told her you'd help. And then you charged her for it! You make me so mad!"

Chelsea swallowed hard. Rob looked ready to

burst. What had happened to her easygoing brother? "I plan to . . ."

Rob cut in with, "You're going to give the money back to Roxie and you're going to apologize to her."

Chelsea had planned to do that very thing, but Rob's attitude made her change her mind. She lifted her chin and glared at him. "You're not my boss, and you can't tell me what to do!" Oh, but she sounded just like Sidney when she talked to Larry! But she wouldn't take back the words. Rob had no right getting mad at her.

"Give back the money, Chelsea! I mean it!"

"I won't do it!" Chelsea doubled her fists and narrowed her eyes. "I'm glad Dad took your computer from you. You were turning into a real nerd!"

"You're one big ugly freckle!" shouted Rob, his face brick-red.

Chelsea ran into the house and slammed the door in Rob's face. How she hated him! She raced upstairs and flung herself across her bed. He was the worst brother in the entire world! How dare he try to boss her around!

7

The Ad

Dad looked around the dinner table with a slight frown. "What's wrong with this family?"

Chelsea almost choked on her bite of pork chop.

Dad put his fork down. "Rob, you're barely eating. Chel, you look like a thundercloud. And, Mike, you have only one good eye."

"I'm staying home tomorrow," said Mom firmly. "I won't leave the children alone after what happened today."

Dad nodded. "It looks like there's more than a swollen eye to deal with." He studied Chelsea, then Rob. "What's up with you two? You act like Sidney and Larry. That's not like you at all."

Chelsea shrugged just as she saw Rob duck his head. She wasn't going to tell Dad anything, and she was glad Rob wouldn't either. Usually they told Dad almost everything.

"Kids, we want you to remember we serve a living God," said Dad. "He knows your hearts. He wants the best for you. And so do your mom and I."

"Your Heavenly Father will always help you," said Mom. "He loves you even more than we do. When you have problems, talk to Him about them. He'll help you find the answers."

The words wrapped around Chelsea's heart, and tears burned the backs of her eyes. She'd always asked God for help in the past. Why wasn't she doing that now?

Dad leaned forward looking very serious. "Kids, we all have an enemy—Satan. He tries his best to ruin our lives. But Jesus has already defeated him! Satan can't ruin our lives unless we let him. God's Spirit lives in us. Greater is He who is in us than he who is in the world! You're victorious through Jesus. Don't forget that when problems come into your life."

Chelsea looked at Rob, and he looked at her. "Sorry," she whispered just as he did the same. They both smiled, and Chelsea felt like a huge weight had lifted off her back.

After dinner and after the dishes were done, Chelsea walked outdoors with Rob. The sun was still warm in the sky. "Rob, I really am sorry. I planned to give Roxie back her money, but you made me mad."

"I'm sorry, too, Chel. I was so surprised you'd

take her money that it made me mad clear through."
Rob laughed. "I sure hate to fight like Sid and
Larry."

"Me too!" Chelsea nodded. "I'll get the money
and give it back to Roxie."

"I already gave it to her. So now you owe it to
me."

"You sure like Roxie, don't you?"

Rob nodded. "She's different than most girls."

Chelsea rolled her eyes. Roxie wasn't kind, but
Chelsea didn't say that. She didn't want Rob mad at
her again. "I'll get the money now. It's in my bank."

After Chelsea gave Rob the money, she found
Mike in the backyard doing his routine. She wanted
to apologize to him too. She waited until his last flip
and said, "Mike, I'm sorry for bumping your arm
before. Will you forgive me?"

"Sure," he said with a shrug. His swollen eye
was partly open, and he looked a little better. "I'm
sorry I got mad at you."

"Are we friends again?" asked Chelsea.

"Sure," said Mike, grinning. "I hope Gavin
comes over, don't you?"

Chelsea flushed and nodded. She was thinking
of Nick.

"I'm gonna see if I can find Gavin's phone number and call him to see if he can come over right
now," said Mike.

Just as Mike slammed the back door, Hannah ran across the street, calling to Chelsea.

Chelsea was surprised Hannah would even speak to her since she'd stayed away from her the past two weeks. She could see Hannah was excited.

"My mom just had a baby boy!" cried Hannah with her hands clasped over her heart. Her dark eyes sparkled. "Our first boy! Four girls and now a boy!"

"That's great," said Chelsea, excited because of Hannah's excitement.

"We named him Burke Shigwam after my dad. Of course, everyone calls my dad Chief. He says his great-great grandfather was an Ottawa chief, so he likes the name."

They talked about names for a while, then Chelsea said, "I'm looking for work. Do you know of anyone who needs help?"

"No. I thought your job was to take care of Mike."

Chelsea told her about the phone bill. "So you see I have to make money fast. If you hear of anything, will you tell me?"

"I have an idea!" Hannah laughed with her head back. "This is really, really great."

"Tell me!" Chelsea sat on the front steps, and Hannah sat beside her.

"You can make an advertisement. You know, a paper that tells what you can do and what hours you can work. Put your name and address and phone number on the paper, then have copies made. We'll pass them out in the neighborhood. You should be able to keep real busy."

Chelsea laughed happily. "You're a genius! When do we start?"

"I could help you make up the ad right now if you want."

"Sure. Let's go to my room and work." Chelsea led the way to her room. She saw the picture of Sidney propped against her phone, and her heart sank. Why did she bring Hannah to her room so they could work together? What had happened to her loyalty to Sidney? Chelsea bit back a groan. First Kathy, now Hannah! Was she so hungry for friends she'd even make friends with Roxie Shoulders?

"You have a pretty room," said Hannah, looking at the mauve-and-blue bedspread and curtains. "I have to share mine with Lena." Hannah wrinkled her nose. "The twins have their own room. Now that we have Burke, I don't know what'll happen. He'll sleep in his crib in Mom and Dad's room for a while, Mom said. Later, I don't know. Mom won't say. Maybe they'll let me make a bedroom in the basement. I've wanted to for a long time. Don't you think that would work?"

Chelsea nodded.

Hannah picked up a rag doll off Chelsea's pillow and hugged her close, then put her back in place. "Our basement has a bathroom. Does yours?"

"Yes."

Hannah clasped her hands over her heart and sank to the bed. "I would love having my own bedroom and my own bathroom!" Suddenly she jumped up. "I came to help you—not talk about a bedroom for me. It's so easy to talk to you, Chelsea!"

Chelsea found it easy to talk to Hannah too, but she didn't say so.

"Where's the paper and the colored markers?" asked Hannah.

Chelsea hesitated, then got out the supplies they needed. Soon she was so involved with working and talking with Hannah, she forgot about feeling loyal to Sidney.

An hour later Mom stuck her head in the doorway and said, "Would you girls like some cookies?"

"Sure!" said Hannah.

"We're having a snack in the kitchen," said Mom. "Come down and join us."

"We'll be right there," Chelsea said. She scooped up the markers and put them away. She hated having a mess. She saw her pile of clothes and decided she'd take care of them before she went to bed. She had been too depressed to do it before. It wasn't like her to have a messy room.

"I'll show this to your family," said Hannah,

picking up the ad they'd finished. "Do you think they'll like it?"

"Yes." Chelsea knew if Rob had his computer he'd design an ad that looked professional. She liked the drawings Hannah had made and the printing she'd done. It was better than professional.

Downstairs Rob pulled up another chair to the kitchen table for Hannah. He even said hello to her.

Chelsea sat on one side of Hannah and Rob the other. Glasses of milk sat at each place, with a napkin to put their cookies on. Mom hated dirty dishes after cleaning the kitchen for the night. Chocolate-chip and M & M cookies covered a large plate beside Mom.

"Does your mother have someone to help with the new baby?" asked Mom as she passed the plate of cookies to Hannah.

"Grandma was supposed to come, but she can't," said Hannah as she took a cookie and passed the plate to Chelsea. "Mom says she doesn't know who to ask. Everybody's so busy."

"I could help off and on during the day." Mom smiled. "I'd like to help with a newborn. It's been a long time since I had a baby."

"Eight years," said Mike, making a face.

"Eight long years," said Dad, chuckling as he ruffled Mike's hair.

"I'll tell Mom," said Hannah.

75

"When will she get home from the hospital?" asked Dad.

"Oh, she didn't go. She had the baby right at home. A midwife came over and delivered the baby. Dad helped."

"Oh my," said Mom, her eyes wide. "I don't know if I could do that."

"Sure you could," said Dad, grinning. "You could do anything you put your mind to."

Mom smiled and sat up a little straighter.

Dad turned to Chelsea and Hannah. "What've you girls been up to?"

Before Chelsea could stop her, Hannah told him and even showed him the ad.

"Good work," said Dad, nodding as he read over the ad. "You should get some results from that." He handed it to Mom to read. "Just make sure you check out the folks you plan to work for. We don't want you to get into any bad situations."

"That's for sure," said Mom, passing the ad to Rob.

"Could I put my name on it too?" asked Rob eagerly. "I have some free time that I could work."

Chelsea bit back a surprised gasp, then nodded. Maybe it had been wise of Dad to take Rob's computer away for the summer.

"Thanks," Rob said with a wide smile.

Hannah looked at the paper again. "You know, I'd like my name on the list too. Chel, you could be the owner of the business, and we'd all work under you. What do you think?"

Chelsea shrugged. She hadn't thought of doing it like that, but it sounded good.

"I think it's a great idea," said Rob. "Between the three of us we could do almost any job."

"I want to have my name on it too," said Mike, eagerly leaning forward. "I want to earn extra money too."

"I don't think there'd be a job for you since you're only eight," said Mom.

Mike's eyes flashed. "I could take a dog for a walk. Or I could help trim weeds from around the sidewalk like I do here."

"You're right," said Dad. "What do you think, Chel? Want to hire Mike on? You're the boss."

The boss! Chelsea sat up straight and lifted her chin. "I say, put his name on the paper."

Mike leaped up with a loud cheer.

Rob frowned thoughtfully. "I think we need a name for our business," he said. "Something catchy and different."

"I have it!" cried Mom, looking ready to burst with excitement. "I read a book when I was a kid about kids who started their own business. They called their business *Kid Power*. But you don't want to copy them, even though it was a good name. I have a better idea!"

"What?" everyone asked at once. Chelsea liked seeing Mom excited.

"*King's Kids*!" said Mom, beaming around the table at everyone. "You all belong to the King of the Universe."

"Great idea," said Dad, and the others agreed.

"*Great or small, we do it all*, can be our slogan," said Rob, as excited as Mom.

"I like it," said Chelsea. This was turning into something bigger than she'd planned.

"We can add the name and the slogan right here," said Hannah, pointing to a blank spot on the paper.

"I'll take the ad to work with me and have copies made as my donation to the cause," said Dad. "Would one hundred be too many?"

"No," said Hannah as Chelsea said, "Yes."

Chelsea gulped. One hundred ads!

"You're the boss," said Hannah. "You decide."

Chelsea shrugged. "I guess we could use that many," she said weakly.

Just then the phone rang, and Mike ran to answer it. "It's probably Gavin," he called over his shoulder.

But when he answered, it was Kathy for Chelsea. "I'll get it in the other room," said Chelsea. She didn't want to talk in the kitchen where everyone could hear her.

In Dad's study she said, "Hi, Kathy."

"Chelsea, you have a job already! If you want it, that is."

Chelsea's stomach cramped, and she leaned weakly against Dad's desk. "What job? Where?"

"Right next door to me! Mrs. Sobol told my mom she needed somebody to clean out her attic and her garage, but she didn't want to pay a fortune for it. I told her about you, and she said to come over in the morning to talk to her about it. Can you come over?"

Chelsea trembled, but said, "I'll be there at nine o'clock sharp."

"Come see me first, and I'll take you over to introduce you. Mrs. Sobol is a little strange. She's all right though. Just strange."

"I'll see you in the morning. Thanks, Kathy."

"What are friends for?"

Chelsea gripped the phone tighter. Were they friends? But not best friends! She'd promised Sidney to be her best friend forever. She couldn't break her word no matter how much she liked Kathy or Kathy liked her.

"See you, Kath." Chelsea slowly hung up, took a deep breath, and walked back to the kitchen. "I got my first job," she said weakly.

8

Brooke Sobol

Chelsea wanted to cling to Kathy's hand as they waited for Mrs. Sobol to answer the door. The house was old and needed painting. The long porch was full of dead leaves and sand and even a broken flowerpot.

"You don't have to be scared of her," said Kathy softly.

Chelsea smiled thankfully. It was as if Kathy could read her mind. "I'm glad you're with me. Rob and Mom are always afraid to meet new people, but I'm usually not. I don't know why today's different."

"Maybe because you need the job so bad," said Kathy.

"You're right!"

"Have you called Sidney again?"

"No. But I wanted to! Especially yesterday after I started the business." Chelsea had picked up the receiver last night to call Sid, then had set it back in place. She couldn't make her bill larger, no matter how badly she needed to talk to Sid!

"I wish my name was on your advertisement," said Kathy wistfully.

"We could add it," said Chelsea. She wished she'd thought about asking Kathy if she wanted to be included.

Kathy sighed heavily and shook her head. Her blonde curls bounced. "I couldn't work anyway. I have to take care of Megan all the time. I sure get tired of watching her."

Just then the door opened, and Brooke Sobol stepped out. She was in her sixties with neatly combed gray hair and brown eyes highlighted with makeup. She wore dark slacks and a flowered blouse and had strands of gold chains hanging around her wrinkled neck onto her chest. "Hello, Kathy." Mrs. Sobol turned to Chelsea. "You must be the one who's going to work for me."

Chelsea nodded.

"I can't remember your name. My memory's not what it once was. Why, at one time I could remember every fourth grader in my class. I was a schoolteacher, you know. Taught close to forty years. I saw everything there was to see in all those years." Mrs. Sobol looked off into space as if she were seeing those things again.

"I'm Chelsea McCrea," said Chelsea hesitantly.

"Chelsea," said Mrs Sobol, blinking her dark eyes. She finally focused on Chelsea. "Now, why are you here?"

"To help clean your attic and garage," said Chelsea as she hooked her red hair behind her ears.

"She's the friend I suggested work for you," said Kathy.

"Yes. From Oklahoma. Now I remember." Mrs. Sobol fingered the chains on her chest. Her hands were as wrinkled as her neck. "When can you start? How much will you charge? How long will it take?"

Chelsea answered the first two questions, then said, "I'll have to see the job to know how long it'll take."

"Then come look." Mrs. Sobol led the way to the two-car garage, puffing as she walked. "I'm not as trim as I used to be." She opened the side door of the garage and stepped inside. An old white Cadillac stood in the spotless stall. In the other stall, boxes surrounded a red dune buggy.

Chelsea's eyes lit up. She wanted to touch the dune buggy and even go for a ride in it.

"I didn't know you had a dune buggy, Mrs. Sobol," said Kathy.

"It belongs to my son Adam. He wanted me to take it to the sand dunes at Lake Michigan and try it out, but I never did get around to it." Mrs. Sobol pushed boxes aside until she reached the dune buggy. She touched it lovingly. "When I was young I rode on a dune buggy with Marshall. We were on our honeymoon." She frowned. "Or was it on our second honeymoon?" She shrugged. "It doesn't matter. We had fun together on a dune buggy. I was so afraid he'd tip it in the sand, but he never did."

Chelsea glanced questioningly at Kathy. What did Mrs. Sobol expect of her?

Suddenly Mrs. Sobol laughed. "I have a marvelous idea, girls! How would you two like a ride on this?" She patted the dune buggy.

Chelsea wanted to say yes, but she said, "I'd love to, but I must get to work."

"And Mom needs me home right away," said Kathy. "I'd love to ride another time."

"So would I," said Mrs. Sobol tearfully. "Time passes so quickly. Marshall is in Heaven. Adam's in Detroit, too busy to visit. And Lissa's in the Rockies in Wyoming. I really should go visit them. Maybe I will today."

Chelsea sucked in air. Wouldn't she be able to get a job after all? She had to pay Dad as soon as possible. He was putting her allowance right onto the bill, and that left her without any money at all.

"What about Chelsea?" asked Kathy, touching Mrs. Sobol's arm.

"Chelsea?" Mrs. Sobol frowned, then her face cleared. "Oh, yes . . . Chelsea. Now, just how long would it take you to stack these boxes neatly against the back of the garage?"

"Not long if they aren't very heavy."

"Oh, they're not. They're empty."

"Empty?" Chelsea bit back a laugh. She didn't dare look at Kathy or she knew they'd both laugh.

"They're packing boxes. I plan to pack up stuff from the attic and get it sent to my children . . . Or somewhere." Mrs. Sobol lifted a box and carried it to the spot where she wanted them stacked. "I planned to do it, but just never got around to it." She fanned herself with her hand. "My but it's hot today. I can't take the heat."

Chelsea carried a box to the back of the garage. "Do you want me to bring the stuff down from the attic?"

"Yes. I have things in piles upstairs. You bring down a pile and pack it, then mark the box *Lissa* or *Adam*. I'll tell you which." Mrs. Sobol carried another box across the garage.

Kathy took the box from her and led her to the door. "You want Chelsea to do that. Why don't you go inside for a cup of tea. You always have tea this time of the morning."

"Yes, I do, don't I?" Mrs. Sobol walked out the door, then stepped back inside. "Chelsea, come look up into the attic in case I'm gone when you start to work there. I want you to know what you'll be doing."

"I'd better get home," said Kathy. "See you later, Chelsea. Bye, Mrs. Sobol. Thanks for giving the job to my friend."

Kathy's *friend*! Chelsea felt warm all over. Like it or not, she and Kathy were friends. Just not best friends, she promised herself as she followed Mrs. Sobol into the large house.

Chelsea liked the big rooms, high ceilings, and heavy doors. She rubbed her hand over the shiny banister as she followed Mrs. Sobol up the wide oak stairs. Everything was neat and clean.

"I might have you clean for me sometime," said Mrs. Sobol over her shoulder. "I get tired cleaning. There's always so much to do."

They walked past bedrooms with beds neatly made and everything dust-free. Mrs. Sobol unlocked and opened a narrow, short door. Heat rushed out along with the smell of mothballs.

"It's an easy walk-in attic," Mrs. Sobol said as she clicked on a light. "I wish there was a window, but there's not. There's a small attic fan that'll help somewhat." She pulled a string dangling down, and a ceiling fan whirred, bringing relief from the heat almost immediately.

Chelsea looked around the dust-free attic. It was much like her Grandma McCrea's attic—filled with odd furniture and clothes.

"This pile of stuff is for Lissa and this one for Adam," said Mrs. Sobol. She looked at the two other piles and shook her head. "Now who are those for?"

"Maybe friends?" suggested Chelsea.

"Maybe. Put them in boxes and label them *Friends*." Mrs. Sobol slowly walked toward the door. "I think I need that cup of tea, then a rest. I'll leave the door unlocked for you and the fan on, but I'll turn off the light."

Chelsea followed Mrs. Sobol back downstairs. "Would you like me to make your tea for you?" asked Chelsea, noticing how weary Mrs. Sobol looked.

"That's very nice of you, dear." Mrs. Sobol led the way to the kitchen, then sank to an oak chair at the round table in the middle of the large room. "The tea kettle already has water in it. Just turn on the fire."

In a few minutes Chelsea had a cup of tea sitting in front of Mrs. Sobol. "Do you want a muffin or something with it?"

"I don't know if I have anything. Look in the fridge and the bread box right there and see."

Chelsea looked in the refrigerator and was alarmed at how empty it was. She opened the bread box and found a pack of muffins, a half-loaf of bread green with mold, and a box of crackers. "Here's a muffin. This bread is spoiled. Where shall I put it?"

"The garbage right there." Mrs. Sobol took out

86

a muffin, then glanced around with a frown. "Now where did I put the butter and jelly?"

Chelsea looked around and finally found a small container of butter, but no jelly.

"I was sure I had some in the fridge," said Mrs. Sobol. She opened the refrigerator, then chuckled. "I forgot to get groceries! No wonder I can't find anything to eat. I'll have to go to the store later."

"Would you like me to go with you?" asked Chelsea, feeling somehow responsible for Mrs. Sobol.

"I can manage, but thanks anyway." Mrs. Sobol took another sip of tea. "You go finish the garage and attic. Find me when you're finished and I'll pay you."

Chelsea didn't want to take money from Mrs. Sobol, but Kathy had assured her the woman could afford to pay for work done.

About an hour later Chelsea finished moving the boxes and sweeping the garage, got a drink of water from the kitchen, then hurried to the attic. Mrs. Sobol wasn't around. Chelsea figured she was resting.

In the attic Chelsea looked around for an easy way to carry down the clothes and odds and ends in each pile. She spotted a medium-sized clothes basket and decided it would work. After several trips she had three boxes full of the things for Lissa. She marked the boxes and taped them shut just as Mrs.

Sobol had said to do. She got another drink of water and slowly walked upstairs. Her legs ached from climbing up and down the steps. Her stomach grumbled with hunger, but she didn't want to go home to eat, then come back. If she hurried, she could finish, then go home to stay.

Her steps became slower and slower as she carried baskets of things to the garage to pack. Just as she started to put a folded shirt into one of Adam's boxes, an envelope fluttered to the garage floor. Chelsea picked it up. "It hasn't even been opened," she muttered in surprise. Mrs. Sobol would probably want to read it. Chelsea pushed it into the back pocket of her jeans, then finished loading the things into the box.

By the time she had only one pile left to load, her legs throbbed and her head spun. She walked to the kitchen for a glass of water. Maybe she should ask Mrs. Sobol if she could finish tomorrow. "Mrs. Sobol," Chelsea called as she walked through the house. Suddenly she realized the Cadillac was gone from the garage. "She went to get groceries probably." Chelsea felt strange in the house all alone. Maybe she could eat a cracker, then go back to work. She felt funny eating the stale cracker, but she knew Mrs. Sobol wouldn't mind.

Upstairs she loaded her basket, then sagged to the floor. She'd rest a while, then finish. She looked around and noticed a foam mattress. She picked up a quilt and spread it over the foam, then eased herself down. She felt as old as Mrs. Sobol.

Chelsea closed her eyes. The room spun, then settled in place. She felt as if she were sinking deep into the mattress and on down into the floor. The whirr of the fan grew fainter and fainter . . .

. . . Suddenly Chelsea sat up. "I fell asleep," she whispered in horror. She jumped up, put the folded quilt back in place, then picked up the basket. She frowned. The attic door was shut. She set the basket down and turned the knob. The door wouldn't budge. She frowned and tried again. Still the door wouldn't open. "Am I locked in?" she asked weakly.

Taking a deep steadying breath, Chelsea knocked on the door. "Mrs. Sobol, can you hear me?" Chelsea's voice cracked. She waited, then knocked again, harder this time. "Mrs. Sobol," she shouted. "Mrs. Sobol!"

Chelsea's stomach knotted. Why would Mrs. Sobol lock her in? "Mrs. Sobol! Please let me out! I'm locked in!"

After several minutes Chelsea realized Mrs. Sobol wasn't coming. Maybe she was still getting groceries. Sometimes Mom took forever to shop. Tears filled Chelsea's eyes, and she sank to the floor near the door and whimpered. The room felt closed in and smelled like sweat and mothballs.

She remembered that the Bible said God was always with her. He was with her even in the locked attic. "Thank You, Heavenly Father, for being with me even here," she whispered with a sob. "I really need Your help. Please send someone to get me out."

She waited, then looked around to see if she could find another way out. There was none. Her heart sank, and sweat broke out on her forehead. Frantically she hammered on the door with her fists. "Mrs. Sobol! Mrs. Sobol!"

"Who's in there?" Mrs. Sobol asked sharply from the other side of the door.

Chelsea's pulse leaped, and she pressed her face close to the door. "It's Chelsea McCrea," she called. "I'm locked in."

Mrs. Sobol unlocked the door and pulled it open. "Oh, my dear, I forgot all about you! I saw the door was unlocked when I came back from getting groceries. Are you alright?"

"Yes." Chelsea nodded as she brushed away her tears.

Mrs. Sobol patted Chelsea's arm. "I'm sorry you were frightened. Come downstairs and get a drink of water and rest a bit."

Chelsea trembled, her legs almost too weak to carry her. She wanted to go home and never return.

In the kitchen Mrs. Sobol handed Chelsea a glass of ice water. "Did you finish your work?"

"Almost," said Chelsea. She drained the glass, thankful for the cold liquid against her dry throat.

"You go home now and come finish tomorrow. I'm sorry about locking you in. It was my bad memory." Mrs. Sobol shook her head and clicked her tongue. "I don't know what's wrong with me. I guess I'm getting old."

Chelsea looked longingly for the door. Finally Mrs. Sobol stopped talking, and Chelsea walked outdoors to her bike. The sun was hot in the sky. A car drove past. A dog barked. Chelsea gripped the handlebars of her bike. Did she really want to come back tomorrow? Maybe she should ask Mrs. Sobol for her pay right now. She looked over her shoulder at the door, then shook her head. No way would she go back inside. Maybe she never would.

9

The Visit

The letter crinkled in her pocket as Chelsea pedaled home. She knew she should turn right around and take it back to Mrs. Sobol. But she just couldn't do it. She had to get home and try to forget how scary it had been to be locked in the attic.

Just as she reached home Mike ran to meet her.

"Guess who's coming here in five minutes?" he asked with a wide grin.

Chelsea wasn't in a guessing mood. "I don't know," she said as she wheeled her bike into the garage, then headed for the door that connected the garage with the laundry room.

"Gavin!" cried Mike, jumping up and down. "And he's bringing a game I don't have!"

Chelsea's heart stopped. "What about Nick? Is he coming too?"

"Sure. He wouldn't let Gavin come alone."

Chelsea's heart leaped, then she looked down at

her dirty shirt and jeans. "I gotta go change!" Suddenly she wasn't bone-weary. Nick was coming!

In her room she peeled off her clothes. The envelope fell to the floor. She picked it up and dropped it beside her telephone. She took a quick shower, pawed through her closet, and finally settled on a pair of blue shorts and a blue T-shirt with tiny flowers around the neckline and sleeves. She brushed her hair and clipped it back with wide blue barrettes. Now she was ready for Nick!

Nonchalantly she walked down the basement stairs. She heard the shouts and laughter of Mike and Gavin. At the bottom of the steps she stopped and looked around. She frowned. Nick wasn't there! She dashed across to Mike and Gavin. She smelled grape gum. "Where's Nick?" she asked, forcing her voice to sound normal.

"He's not here," said Mike, not taking his eyes off the game.

Gavin twisted around and looked up at Chelsea. "He dropped me off and left. He'll be back for me in an hour."

"Oh," Chelsea said as she backed slowly away. "Did he . . . ask about me?"

"Yeah, but Mike said you ran away when you heard he was coming."

Chelsea bit back angry words as she turned and raced upstairs. How could Mike be so stupid? She dashed into the kitchen and almost slammed into Mom.

"What's wrong, Chel?" asked Mom, catching Chelsea's arms. "You look upset. How did it go with Mrs. Sobol?"

Chelsea struggled with blurting out her anger at Mike for telling Nick she'd run away. Instead she told Mom about Mrs. Sobol and about getting locked in the attic.

"Oh, honey, I'm sorry! I know how frightened you must've been." Mom pulled Chelsea close and held her.

Chelsea leaned against Mom, glad for her mother's warm arms around her. She smelled a faint whiff of rose perfume.

"Thank God you're all right," said Mom, smiling as she held Chelsea away from her to look into her face. "I'm glad you remembered to pray. Always *always* remember to call on God in any situation."

"I'll try," Chelsea whispered.

"I was just on my way to the Shigwams. Would you like to go with me and see the baby? Oh, Chelsea, he's beautiful! And Beryl is doing just fine. She's already up and about after having the baby just yesterday. It's incredible." Mom tugged Chelsea's hand. "Come see him and meet Beryl."

Chelsea agreed. Maybe she'd be able to talk to Hannah a while.

A few minutes later after meeting Beryl

Shigwam, Chelsea sat in the living room with the tiny baby in her arms. He was wrapped in a lightweight blue blanket and wore a blue sleeper. He smelled like baby powder. His hair was black and his face red. His tiny fingers were perfect, with perfect little fingernails. He was the cutest baby she'd ever seen. Her heart swelled as she felt his warmth against her. "He's adorable." Chelsea smiled at Hannah, sitting beside her on the couch.

"I know," said Hannah proudly.

"Where are your little sisters?" asked Chelsea.

"Mom's friend took them to her house for the day just to make it easier on Mom." Hannah sighed heavily. "I wish somebody would take me home and make it easier on me."

"Come home with me," said Chelsea.

"I wish I could, but Mom needs me here." Hannah rubbed Burke's black hair. "I didn't want a baby brother or sister when Mom first told me, but after I held Burke I was happy to have him. He's just so much work! And he cried a lot last night."

"I'm sorry," said Chelsea. She didn't know what else to say.

Burke squirmed in Chelsea's arms, and she carefully handed him to Hannah. Hannah laid him on his stomach in his little carry basket on the floor next to the couch. He squirmed and made little whimpering sounds, then was quiet.

"Tell me about your first job," said Hannah eagerly.

Chelsea told her. She'd forgotten to tell her Mom about the letter she'd found, but she remembered it now and mentioned it to Hannah.

"Maybe it's an important mystery letter," said Hannah. "Was it *to* Mrs. Sobol or *from* her?"

Chelsea shrugged. "I didn't notice. But it's on my desk at home. I'll look when I get there."

"I love mysteries!"

"Maybe it's no mystery at all," Chelsea said with a grin. "You could be getting excited over nothing."

"You're right. I do that sometimes." Hannah laced her fingers together. "But what if it is a mystery? Please, let me help solve it if it is! Please!"

Chelsea laughed and nodded. "I will." Before she knew it, she was telling Hannah about Nick Rand taking his brother to her house. "I don't want him to think I ran away from him," she said with a long sigh.

"Just be there when he picks Gavin up. Be friendly with him. Ask him what interests him." Hannah's eyes twinkled as she rattled off Chelsea's rules on how to make friends.

Chelsea giggled, and Hannah joined in. Before long they were laughing so hard they couldn't talk. Chelsea forgot about being reserved around

Hannah. She didn't think about Sidney and the times they'd giggled until their sides ached at all.

Several minutes later Chelsea sat on her front steps and waited for Nick. Her hands felt clammy, and butterflies fluttered in her stomach. Maybe Nick would call her Freckles again and not want to be friends.

Just then Nick rode up on his bike, parked it near the garage beside Gavin's, and waved to her. He wore gray-and-blue shorts and a blue T-shirt.

She waved back at him, then walked slowly toward him. "Hi," she said. Was that all she could say?

"Hi." Nick smiled. "I'm glad Mike can open his eye again."

"Me too." Her paper on how to make friends flashed before her as well as what Hannah had said. What would interest Nick? A dune buggy? "Did you ever ride on a dune buggy?" she blurted out.

"A couple of times," he said as they walked to the steps and sat down. "Have you?"

"No, but I'd like to." She told him about Mrs. Sobol's dune buggy and her offer to take them for a ride. Soon she was talking as easily to Nick as she did with Hannah or Kathy. She even told him about working to pay the phone bill.

"I'll tell Mom about you," said Nick, smiling. "Sometimes when I'm gone she needs somebody to watch Gavin. You'd be good with Gavin because of your watching Mike."

Chelsea flushed. "But I let Mike get a black eye."

"No, he did that. He was trying to pick a fight, and Gavin was glad to fight. He's always ready for one."

"Are you?"

"No. I'd rather work on my computer."

"You would? So does Rob, my other brother." Chelsea jumped up. "Come on! I'll introduce you to him. He's in the kitchen having a snack."

In the kitchen Rob looked up from the bowl of Cheerios he was eating at the table.

"Rob, this is Nick Rand, Gavin's brother. Nick has a computer too."

Nick sat down, and he and Rob exchanged computer information while Chelsea listened with interest. After a few minutes she was bored. She tried to speak, but the boys were too involved with their talk to even notice her. Finally she walked upstairs to her room, her steps slow and her head down.

Listlessly she picked up the letter she'd inadvertently brought home from Mrs. Sobol's. She might as well check it out so she could tell Hannah what she'd learned. The letter was addressed to Mrs. Sobol. The postmark was March. *Three months ago,* reflected Chelsea. The return address didn't have a name, only an address. *Maybe I should take this back to her now.* Just the thought of talking to Mrs. Sobol again made her change her mind. Mrs. Sobol was strange! Kathy had said she was, but she'd also said she was alright. Maybe she should call Kathy and tell her about the letter.

Chelsea glanced at the phone. The picture of Sidney seemed to jump out at her. "Oh, Sid! I miss you so much!" She desperately wanted to tell Sid all that had happened today. Sid would understand how it felt being locked in the attic. She'd been locked in the bathroom for almost an hour when she was four. To this day she hated being behind locked doors.

A yearning to see Sid rose in Chelsea, and tears burned her eyes. She knew she couldn't see Sid, but she could talk to her. Maybe she could call just one more time. "Just a quick call," she whispered.

Just then the phone rang, and Chelsea jumped and shrieked. She laughed self-consciously as she reached to answer it. It was Mrs. Rand to see if her boys had started home yet; if not, she needed them home immediately.

"They're still here," said Chelsea. "But I'll tell them you called."

Breathing a sigh of relief that Mrs. Rand had stopped her from calling Sid, Chelsea ran to the kitchen. Rob and Nick were still talking computers. "Sorry to bother you, Nick, but your mom called. She wants you and Gavin home now."

Nick jumped up with a gasp. "I forgot the time! I gotta go."

Chelsea followed him to the basement stairs

and waited while he called Gavin. "I hope nothing's wrong," she said.

"Don't worry about it." Nick smiled.

"If you're sure." She saw a worried look in his eyes, but didn't ask anything else. "Will you come again?"

"Sure. And Rob said he'd be over to see me. He wants to see a new game I have. And he wants to see my design program."

Chelsea's heart sank. Nick never once mentioned her coming over or him coming back to see her.

A few minutes later she stood in the yard with Rob and watched Nick and Gavin ride away. She sighed heavily. Maybe she should learn more about computers.

"I like Nick," said Rob. "He knows as much about computers as I do."

Chelsea's jaw tightened. "Whoop-tee-do," she said.

"Are you mad at me?" asked Rob in surprise.

Chelsea glared at him. "Why should I be?"

"I don't know." Rob spread his hands wide. "I don't know you any more, Chel! You're always mad."

"Always? I'm not always mad!" she shouted, doubling her fists at her sides. "You're the one who's different. But then everything is! I hate Michigan! I want to go home!" She burst into tears, then ran to the house before anyone saw her cry.

10

Another Phone Call

Chelsea looked at the one hundred brightly colored copies of her ad that Dad had put in her hands. "There are ... so ... many," she said weakly.

"You'll have a great time passing them out," said Dad, winking at her. "You have friends and family who'll be glad to help you."

She didn't know about that, especially if she kept making Rob and Mike angry at her. She rubbed a hand over the copies. "What if everybody wants me at once?"

"You have others under you," said Dad with a hearty laugh as he slipped off his gray suit coat. "You're the president of *King's Kids*. You can assign each person a job to do."

"There's always the chance that nobody will hire you to do anything," said Rob.

Chelsea wanted to walk away from Dad's smile and Rob's frown, but she knew it was time to sit down to dinner. So she laid the copies of her ad on the kitchen counter and walked over to the already-set table. Smells of roast beef, mashed potatoes, buttered broccoli, and hot rolls filled the kitchen. Chelsea didn't think she could eat a bite, but she found that after such a long day she was *starving*.

Just after the kitchen was cleaned Dad said, "Since it's such a beautiful evening, let's go for a walk. The park has a great trail for hikes."

"Hiking!" cried Mike, walking on his hands across the kitchen.

Chelsea turned away before Dad saw her frown. She did not want to go on a hike with the family now or any other time. She wanted to go back home to Oklahoma where she belonged!

Mom hugged Dad. "A hike! How wonderful! I'll change my shoes and be right back."

"Could I see if Roxie wants to go?" asked Rob as he tied his left sneaker.

"Not this time," said Dad. "This will be family time. Maybe next time. We want to do this regularly."

"Yahoo!" shouted Mike. "I'll see if I can run all the way around the trail without stopping."

Chelsea wanted to see if she could get out of going, but she knew it wouldn't do any good to ask. "I'll wait outdoors," she said.

Slowly she walked around the house. It was seven o'clock but still as light out as at noontime.

The sun was warm, and a gentle breeze blew smells of flowers to her. She saw Hannah step outdoors, then go quickly back inside. Probably the baby had started crying.

"Are you still mad at me?" asked Rob behind Chelsea.

She whirled around. "No! Just leave me alone!"

Rob shrugged. "I wanted to tell you that Sidney called just now."

"What! Why didn't you come get me?"

"She said she had to hang up quick because her mom had just walked in. She wasn't supposed to be calling, but she said she had to talk to you."

Chelsea started for the house, but Mom, Dad, and Mike stepped out. Dad locked the door behind him. Chelsea trembled. She had to call Sid and see what was wrong. It had to be something terrible since Sid was willing to disobey her mom by calling.

"Let's go," shouted Dad as if he were leading a march. He held Mom's hand, and they swung their hands between them. "What a great evening for a walk. Breathe that fresh air!"

Chelsea fell into step behind everyone. Mike ran on ahead, shouting back that he'd beat them all to the park. Gracie ran after Mike, barking at his heels. She finally gave up and trotted for home. Chelsea watched to see if she ran into Roxie's yard, but she didn't. Maybe Roxie had found a way to keep Gracie out of their flowers.

At the park Chelsea looked up at the tall trees on either side of the trail covered with wood chips. Branches almost met overhead and blocked out the bright rays of the sun. Families walked ahead of and behind them. Joggers passed them, keeping to the side of the trail. A baby in a stroller jabbered, making his parents laugh as they pushed him along.

Someone touched Chelsea's arm, and she jumped in surprise. She turned her head to find Kathy Aber there. "Kathy!"

"My family's here on a walk too," said Kathy, smiling. "I'd like you to meet all of them." Her family stopped just as Chelsea's parents turned around.

"So you're Kathy. I'm Glenn McCrea." Chelsea's dad smiled at Kathy and her family. "This is my wife Billie, our son Rob, and up ahead there is Mike."

"I'm Tommy Aber," said Kathy's dad. Chelsea stared at him. He had a long blond ponytail and wore jeans with a tear in the knee and a bright red T-shirt with *I Write Music* written in black across it. "This is my wife Grace, our son Duke, you know Kathy, and our baby, Megan."

"I'm not a baby," said Megan, shaking her head hard.

"You're *our* baby," said Grace Aber. She was

short and plump and wore a big pink shirt that hung over khaki-colored baggy shorts.

Chelsea and Kathy hung back while their families paired off, talking as if they'd always known each other. Chelsea was amazed that Rob talked to Duke. Megan tried to catch Mike, but he always stayed a few feet in front of her.

"What happened with Mrs. Sobol today?" asked Kathy in a low voice as they followed their families. "She came over all upset, but I had to take Megan out to the sandbox, so I couldn't hear."

"She accidentally locked me in the attic," said Chelsea, shivering as she thought about it.

"That's terrible! No wonder she was so upset." Kathy shook her head.

"I'm supposed to go back tomorrow and finish."

"Good! Maybe we can talk a while."

"I don't know if I want to go back," whispered Chelsea.

"But you must! Mrs. Sobol would feel terrible if you didn't."

"But what if she locks me in again?"

"I'll check on you and make sure she doesn't."

Chelsea sighed. "All right, I'll go. I have a letter to give her anyway." She told Kathy about the letter as they fell further and further behind their families.

"Where was it from?" asked Kathy eagerly.

"I can't remember. I looked at the address, but I didn't really pay attention."

Her eyes bright with excitement, Kathy gripped Chelsea's arm. "Maybe it's from her sister Pearl Phiffer. They've been in a fight the last five years. Mrs. Phiffer called Dad one night last week and asked about Mrs. Sobol. She said she'd written and her sister wouldn't answer her—not her letters or her phone calls. She was afraid something had happened to her. Dad said she was fine. So he asked Mrs. Sobol about Mrs. Phiffer. Mrs. Sobol got very upset and said she didn't want anyone to talk to her about her sister. Dad tried, but she wouldn't listen at all. We've been praying for them. It's terrible to stay angry."

Chelsea looked down at the wood chips. She'd been angry at Dad since he'd said they had to move. And now she was angry with Rob.

"Jesus wants us to love each other, not be angry," said Kathy. She lowered her voice. "I have to remember that a lot because of Megan."

Chelsea didn't want to think about her anger, so she quickly changed the subject and talked about the hundred copies of her ad she had to pass out.

Laughing, Kathy skipped a few steps ahead of Chelsea, then back beside her. "Tomorrow afternoon Dad is taking Megan to play with a friend! I'll help you then!"

"Thanks, Kathy. Hannah said she'd help too if

she can." Chelsea told Kathy about Hannah's new baby brother. "I got to hold him. He's so cute!"

"I love babies," said Kathy. "When I get married I want three babies—two boys and a girl. And the girl will be the youngest so she never has to baby-sit her brothers."

Later at home Chelsea said good night to her family and walked slowly upstairs. She had to be at Mrs. Sobol's by 9, so she wanted to get right to sleep.

She opened her windows and let the cool breeze blow in. Back home they'd have the air on and not be able to open the windows because of the heat outdoors. She slipped on her big Oklahoma T-shirt that reached to her knees. How she wanted to go back! She picked up Sidney's picture and held it against her heart. "I miss you, Sid. Did you call me because you miss me?"

Chelsea reached for the phone, then jerked her hand back. She'd promised she wouldn't make any more long-distance calls.

In the bathroom she brushed her teeth, made a face at her freckles, then ran down the hall to her room. She knew Mike and Rob were already in bed. Mom and Dad were in the kitchen talking over cups of tea. Dad had said he wanted to read a while, then he and Mom would hit the hay. He always said that when he meant they were going to sleep.

In her room Chelsea slipped between her

sheets. The light coming through her windows bathed her room in a soft light. She closed her eyes, then opened them. What had Sidney wanted? What if something dreadful had happened? Sidney must have needed to talk to her badly in order to call.

"I can't call her," whispered Chelsea, once again closing her eyes. She remembered the time Sid had accidentally broken her family's picture window and had come crying to her for help. She thought of the time Sid had won first prize in a coloring contest and had run to show her the prize before she showed it to anyone else. "Oh, Sidney, I miss you!"

Chelsea glanced at her desk. The light shone on Sid's picture, making Chelsea miss her even more. "I have to call her! I have to!"

Chelsea slipped out of bed, then frowned, her heart thundering. Mom and Dad always looked in when they went past her open door. What if they looked in while she was on the phone? Oh, it would be too awful!

Quickly she bunched her pillows up and tucked them between her sheets to make it look like she was still in bed. She put her rag doll next to the pillows.

Her hand trembling, she carried the phone away from the desk and sat on the floor with it. She pulled her Oklahoma T-shirt over her knees and quickly rang Sidney's house. Sid answered on the first ring. The sound of Sid's voice brought tears to Chelsea's eyes.

"Hi, Sid," said Chelsea, brushing a tear off her cheek.

"I thought it'd be you," said Sid. "I am *so* glad you called!"

"Rob told me you phoned earlier. I wish I could've talked to you then."

"Me too."

"You won't believe how terrible it is here," said Chelsea.

"It's terrible here without you," said Sid.

Chelsea's eyes widened. "What about Megan?"

"That's why I called you! I had to talk to someone, and I knew you'd listen. You can't believe what she did to me!"

Chelsea bit her lip to keep from crying out in pain. Sid wanted to talk about Megan! Chelsea tasted blood and quickly released her lip. She wanted to tell Sid she was hanging up now, but Sidney kept talking about how Megan wanted to go to the mall and she wanted to go swimming.

"And Megan always thinks we have to do what *she* says!" cried Sidney. "I wanted to go swimming. It's 95 degrees out, Chel! It's perfect for swimming. And I didn't have a dime to spend at the mall. I already spent more than I should when we went the last time. But Megan won't listen. She doesn't even care! I thought we were friends, but we aren't. Nobody's as good a friend as you, Chel. You know that, don't you? You're my very best friend, and you always will be. I'm not even going to talk to Megan again. I won't sleep over at her house anymore, and I won't invite her here. I mean it! Chel, you're my best friend."

Chelsea's heart swelled with happiness. "Sid, you're my very best friend too! I mean it!"

"I thought you said you made two friends . . . Hannah and Kathy."

"Oh, them! They're barely friends, Sid." Chelsea flushed as she said it. She knew Hannah and Kathy would be hurt badly if they knew she'd said such a terrible thing. "I would never give you up. Never!"

"I'm so glad, Chel! I'd hate to have any best friend except you. I have so much to tell you. Did I tell you Paul Ellison stopped over again here? He said he wanted to see Larry, but I knew he came to talk to me. You can just tell sometimes." Sid giggled, and Chelsea giggled too.

"And I memorized the most Bible verses in Sunday school the last two weeks." Sid told Chelsea all the details of the contest and who'd almost beat her.

Chelsea told Sidney about Mrs. Sobol and even about Nick.

"I'm going to find jobs just the way you are," said Sid excitedly. "I mean it! I'll hand out ads and get jobs and make enough money to buy my own school clothes this year. I already know exactly what sneakers I want. You'd love them too, Chel."

Chelsea listened as Sid told her about the shoes and the other clothes she wanted. While Sid was talking, Chelsea heard a noise in the hallway. Her heart stopped, then pounded so hard in her ear she couldn't hear Sidney.

Dad and Mom stopped at Chelsea's door, whispered a minute, then walked away.

Sweat popped out on Chelsea's forehead. She had almost been caught! Then it hit her. She would be caught anyway—when the bill came next month. She groaned and bent almost double. She tried twice to break in on Sidney, then finally said, "Sid, stop talking! I have to hang up right now!"

"Please don't, Chel. Please!"

"I must. Do you know how much this'll cost? I have to go." Chelsea said a quick good-bye and with a trembling hand hung up the receiver. She set the phone back on her desk and crept between the sheets, pushing her rag doll to the carpeted floor.

"What have I done?" muttered Chelsea into her pillow. She closed her eyes tight, turned on her side, and lay there thinking about the bill she'd just made. But worse than the bill was her disobedience.

Hot tears slipped from under her lashes and wet her cheeks.

11

The Missing Dune Buggy

Chelsea could barely swallow her Cheerios. She'd already overslept and would be late for work, but she still couldn't manage to get going. Thinking of last night made her tremble and almost drop her spoon. Oh, why had she disobeyed? She knew better, yet she'd done it anyway. She'd almost always obeyed before. What had made her disobey this time? Her head spun so much she couldn't find the answer.

Mom leaned over Chelsea and kissed her on the head. "I love you, honey. And I'm proud of you."

The words burned into Chelsea. Mom wouldn't be proud of her or love her if she knew she'd disobeyed.

"I know you'll do a good job today," said Mom. "I'll see you later. And I plan to help you pass out your ads this afternoon."

"Thanks," said Chelsea, choking back a sob. How she wanted to throw her arms around Mom and confess what she'd done!

"I've got to get busy," said Mom, heading for the laundry room. "I forgot to tell you . . . I'll need you to watch Mike tomorrow morning."

Chelsea nodded. She'd do anything to feel better.

"See you later."

Chelsea opened her mouth to call Mom back, but she snapped it closed. She *couldn't* tell her. She would make enough money to pay last night's bill, and she'd never ever make another long-distance call. And she'd be so good she wouldn't even *consider* disobeying! Even after that decision she felt terrible inside.

At Mrs. Sobol's house Chelsea rang the doorbell, then waited. "Oh, no," she muttered. "I forgot the letter!" Now she'd have to come again just to return the letter. She'd planned to finish quickly and never see Mrs. Sobol again.

The door opened, and Mrs. Sobol said, "I was afraid you wouldn't come again, Chelsea. Please *please* forgive me for locking you in the attic. I even had a nightmare about it. But you were my sister when I let you out." Mrs. Sobol looked closely at Chelsea. "You're not Pearl, are you?"

"No. I'm Chelsea McCrea."

"I can see that. Pearl doesn't have red hair and

freckles." Mrs. Sobol stepped back with the door opened wide. "Come in and get your work finished. I have things to do and people to see."

Chelsea flushed as she hurried upstairs to the attic. She carried down the already-packed basket and finished filling a box that was marked *Friends*.

There was something different about the garage. She looked around with a thoughtful frown. Then she realized what it was. The dune buggy was gone! Had Mrs. Sobol sold it?

Just then Mrs. Sobol walked into the garage. She stopped short, and her face turned ashen. She clutched at her wrinkled throat. "What did you do with the dune buggy?"

"Me!" cried Chelsea, jumping back. "It was gone when I came in!" How could Mrs. Sobol think she'd take the dune buggy?

"Did you drive it out?" asked Mrs. Sobol, rushing to look in the driveway outside the garage.

"I can't even drive!" cried Chelsea, running beside Mrs. Sobol.

"Then where did it go?" Mrs. Sobol spun on Chelsea. "Did you tell anyone it was here?"

"Well . . . yes, I did." She'd told her family, Nick, Hannah, and even Sidney. "But none of them would take your dune buggy!"

"I must call the police! I must get the dune buggy back. It belongs to Adam. What would he do

if he knew someone stole it right out of my garage?"
Mrs. Sobol looked ready to fall over.

Chelsea caught her arm and led her to a bench
outside the garage. "Sit down for a while."

Just then Kathy ran up to them. "Is something
wrong? Are you sick, Mrs. Sobol?"

"Somebody stole the dune buggy," she said, her
eyes filling with tears. "I think Chelsea did it."

Chelsea shook her head hard. "I didn't. I really
didn't. You know I wouldn't, don't you, Kathy?"

"Of course," said Kathy, smiling reassuringly
at Chelsea. "Mrs. Sobol doesn't really think you
stole it—do you, Mrs. Sobol? Chelsea's here to help
you, not to take your dune buggy."

"I don't trust her," said Mrs. Sobol.

"Tell her you wouldn't take anything of hers,"
said Kathy.

Chelsea flushed, making her freckles blend into
one red mass.

"She looks guilty to me!" cried Mrs. Sobol,
pushing herself up and shaking her finger at Chelsea.
"Out with it, girl! What did you take?"

Chelsea swallowed hard. A butterfly flew past
and landed on a yellow marigold. Chelsea twisted a
strand of red hair around her finger. "A letter."

"See? I told you. If she'd take a letter, she'd take
a dune buggy!"

Kathy looked toward her house. "I'll get Dad,"
she said softly to Chelsea.

Chelsea wanted to beg her not to go, but she knew they couldn't handle Mrs. Sobol alone.

"Just what letter did you take?" asked Mrs. Sobol sharply.

Chelsea blinked back scalding tears. She pushed her trembling hands into the pockets of her jeans. "I found it in Adam's stuff."

"A letter in Adam's stuff! And you took it! I'm calling the police right now!"

"No, wait! I meant to give it to you, but I forgot when you locked me in the attic."

His blond ponytail flipping around wildly, Tommy Aber ran into the yard with Kathy. He wore cutoffs and a blue-and-pink tie-dyed T-shirt. "Mrs. Sobol, what's this about your dune buggy?"

"Tommy, this girl took a letter from me, and if she'd do that she'd take my dune buggy."

Tommy shook his head and helped Mrs. Sobol to the bench. "Kathy, run in and get her a glass of water."

"I *am* thirsty," said Mrs. Sobol as Kathy ran off. "I always get a dry mouth when I get excited."

Chelsea moved from one foot to the other. She wanted to leap on her bike and ride like the wind back to Oklahoma.

Tommy smiled at Chelsea. "I know there's a logical explanation about the dune buggy. Relax—we'll get it all sorted out."

Chelsea felt a little better. In first grade she'd

been accused of stealing Polly Goulder's milk, but she was as innocent then as she was now.

A minute later Kathy handed Mrs. Sobol the glass of water, then stood beside Chelsea. "Don't worry," she whispered. "Remember, God is with you."

Chelsea bit her lip. How could God be with her after she'd disobeyed her parents?

Mrs. Sobol drank half the glass of water, then held it out to Kathy. "Thank you. I do feel much better."

Tommy patted Mrs. Sobol's wrinkled hand. "Did you perhaps loan out the dune buggy?" he asked softly. "Did someone come here and want to take it to Sleeping Bear Dunes?"

Mrs. Sobol gasped. "Yes! Last night Adam called me and said his friend Joe Smythe was stopping in to use the dune buggy. Adam gave Joe his set of keys. Yes, that's right—Joe borrowed the dune buggy! He said he'd bring it back after the weekend."

"There," said Tommy, smiling. "It's all settled."

Mrs. Sobol held her hand out to Chelsea. "Please forgive me for accusing you. I am sorry. Really, I'm very sorry."

Chelsea wanted to get out of there, but she had to get her pay, so she nodded.

"Did you finish your work?" asked Tommy.

"Almost," said Chelsea.

"Kathy, help Chelsea finish, will you? I'll sit a while with Mrs. Sobol."

"Hold it!" cried Mrs. Sobol. "What about the letter?"

Chelsea trembled. "I could get it right now."

"No, finish your work first, then get it," said Mrs. Sobol.

With Kathy beside her, Chelsea ran into the garage, picked up the basket, and hurried to the attic.

"Please be patient with Mrs. Sobol," said Kathy as they worked. "I love her. She wasn't always this way, but since she and her sister had their terrible fight, she's changed. And she gets worse every day."

Chelsea shuddered. Would that happen with her if she continued to fight with Rob and Mike? She forced back the thought as they worked fast. In fifteen minutes they were done.

"I'll share my pay with you, Kathy," Chelsea said as they left the garage.

"Not a chance," said Kathy, shaking her head. "I wanted to help you and Mrs. Sobol. But now I have to get home. Will you be alright?"

"Yes."

"I'll talk to you later." Kathy waved good-bye to Mrs. Sobol and ran home.

Chelsea got her bike and wheeled it to Mrs. Sobol's side. "I'll be right back with the letter."

"Here's your pay first," snapped Mrs. Sobol, holding a sealed envelope out to Chelsea.

"Thank you," said Chelsea weakly as she stuffed the envelope in her pocket. "I'll be right back." She wheeled around a white cat ambling past, then pedaled fast for home. Hot wind whipped her long hair back. In the distance a siren wailed.

In her room she pulled the envelope from her pocket and opened it. There was a fifty dollar bill inside! She groaned and shook her head. Mrs. Sobol had probably thought she put in a five dollar bill.

"I should keep it, after what she put me through," muttered Chelsea, scowling. But she knew she couldn't. That would be stealing. She stuffed it back in her pocket and picked up Mrs. Sobol's letter.

Back at Mrs. Sobol's she handed the sealed letter to her. The woman was sitting in the kitchen eating a peanut butter and jelly sandwich and drinking a glass of milk. "I also brought back the envelope you gave me." Chelsea dropped it on the table.

"Didn't I pay you enough?" asked Mrs. Sobol sharply.

Chelsea bit back her anger. "You accidentally put a fifty dollar bill in there."

"A fifty? Never!"

Chelsea pulled the bill out and dropped it beside Mrs. Sobol's glass of milk. "That is a fifty dollar bill."

Mrs. Sobol picked it up, shaking her head. "So it is. So it is." She opened a cupboard door and pulled out another envelope. "This is probably yours. That's my grocery money."

Chelsea opened the envelope and found fifteen dollars inside. She nodded. "This is mine. Thank you."

"And thank you for being honest." Mrs. Sobol patted her cheeks with a tissue. "I feel bad about yelling at you and accusing you of stealing. How can I repay you?"

Chelsea looked at the unopened letter. To her surprise she really wanted to know what it was. Hannah would want to know too. "Tell me who your letter is from."

Mrs. Sobol shrugged. "I guess I can do that." She ripped it open, looked it over, then tossed it to the floor. "From Pearl! I should've known she'd try something funny. She had someone else address the envelope so I wouldn't recognize the handwriting."

Chelsea picked up the letter. "Why won't you read it?"

"No need. It's only more lies!" snapped Mrs. Sobol.

"Maybe she wants to make up." Chelsea couldn't believe she was saying that. Maybe she was trying to make up for her own anger and disobedience. She wanted to do something to help Mrs.

Sobol. Besides, it would be terrible to go through life not remembering things.

"She does not want to make up!" Mrs. Sobol took a bite of her sandwich and chewed it as if it were made of rubber.

Chelsea felt she had to help settle the fight between Mrs. Sobol and her sister to make up for the bad things she'd done. "I'll read it to you since you don't want to touch it or read it yourself."

Mrs. Sobol thought a while and finally shrugged. "I could still say I never read it and I wouldn't be lying."

"That's right." Chelsea opened the letter and read, "'Dear Brooke, I wish you'd answer my letters or talk to me on the phone. I am finally going to give in and come live with you.'"

"What?" Mrs. Sobol grabbed the letter. "'. . . give in and come live with you. I will be there by the end of June, so be ready for me. If you've changed your mind now that you're angry with me, I'll have to sleep on the street. I've sold my house and must be out by the end of June.'" Mrs. Sobol shook her head. "Lies! She wants me to get ready for her to come, then call and say she changed her mind. She did that five years ago, and I won't put up with her doing it again."

"Call her and see if she's serious," said Chelsea.

"How would I know if she's telling the truth?"

Chelsea thought a while. "Find out if she sold

the house. Like from the real estate company or something."

"You're quite a detective, aren't you? I'll do that!" Mrs. Sobol walked to the phone hanging on the wall near the back door. She looked up a number and dialed it.

"I should get home," said Chelsea, but she sat at the table with her chin in her hands as Mrs. Sobol talked on the phone.

Mrs. Sobol finally hung up and sank back down on her chair. "She sold the house," she whispered. "She really is going to move in with me."

"Are you glad?"

"Of course! That's what I wanted all along, but she said she couldn't put up with me. Well, I can't put up with her either, but we *are* sisters, and we should spend the rest of our days together." Mrs. Sobol slapped her forehead. "That means I have to get a bedroom ready for her. Chelsea, I'll need you to work longer for me. I have only three days to get ready for Pearl."

Chelsea thought a while and finally nodded. Now that she knew what kind of woman Mrs. Sobol was, she could work for her without being afraid. Besides, she desperately needed the money. "I'll take the job," said Chelsea.

"Start in the morning at 9."

"I'll have to bring my little brother with me. Mom's looking for a job, and she has an interview."

"What's his name?"

"Mike. He's eight."

"Bring him. I'll put him to work."

Chelsea smiled. "He'll like that." She ran to her bike and pedaled toward home. She tried to laugh, but couldn't. Why was her heart still so heavy after what she'd done to help Mrs. Sobol?

12

Hard Work

Chelsea held the stack of ads in her hand. They smelled like a copy machine. How she hated to go door to door passing them out! Mom and Mike had already taken a bundle in the car with them to pass out on the far side of The Ravines.

Just then Roxie Shoulders ran into the yard. Her short dark hair was brushed back from her round face. Her wide brown eyes twinkled. "I'll help you with those," she said, pointing to the ads. "Rob told me about them."

Chelsea backed away, shaking her head. "You don't have to help." She wanted to say, "We don't even like each other."

"But I want to because you helped with the flowers." Roxie reached for the ads. "Rob and I are going to pass them out together."

Reluctantly Chelsea handed Roxie a batch.

"Besides, I want my name added to the list of

King's Kids. Rob said you're the boss, but that you'd probably let me in if I asked."

A muscle jumped in Chelsea's jaw. She wanted to yell at Roxie, but she quietly said, "I'll add you to the list."

"Thank you." Roxie moved restlessly. She tugged her brightly flowered T-shirt over her red shorts. "I'm sorry about your phone bill."

"Yes . . . Well, so am I." Chelsea was surprised at Roxie's words. She had thought Roxie would gloat over anything bad in Chelsea's life. Maybe she wasn't so terrible after all.

Rob ran out the back door and around to Roxie and Chelsea. "I'm ready," he said as he hiked up his jeans.

Chelsea stared in surprise at Rob. Was this the same shy boy who hid in his room with his computer? He actually had a suntan! He talked to Roxie as if she were one of the family and not a stranger.

"We'll pass out the ads on the streets I marked a while ago," said Rob. They'd made a plan on where to pass out ads so they wouldn't go to the same place twice.

Chelsea nodded speechlessly. She watched them walk away, talking happily to each other.

Barking wildly, Gracie ran into the yard, chasing a white cat. The cat streaked away, and Gracie ran into Roxie's yard. Chelsea dashed after Gracie and shooed her away from the flowers. Slowly

Chelsea walked to her yard. "I can't believe I saved the flowers for Roxie," she muttered, shaking her head. "But I'm glad I did."

Chelsea looked down at the ads in her hands and wrinkled her nose. It was harder to pass out the ads than it was to work all day long for Mrs. Sobol.

Just as she started down the sidewalk, Kathy rode up on her bike and Hannah ran across the street.

"Chelsea!" they both called at once.

Chelsea's heart leaped, then she frowned. Last night she'd again promised Sidney to be her best friend. She'd said Hannah and Kathy were barely friends. Well, she'd keep it that way no matter how nice they were. "Hi," she said stiffly.

"I came to help," they said at the same time, then laughed.

"You don't need to," said Chelsea, shaking her head. How could she keep them at a distance if they kept being so nice and helpful?

"I can only do my block," said Hannah, "because I can't be gone long." She pulled several ads from Chelsea's hand. "I have to hurry." She smiled and ran back across the street to start to work.

"And I'll go with you, Chelsea," said Kathy. "I know it's hard for you to do this."

Chelsea blinked back tears. How did Kathy know? Not even Sidney would've known unless she'd told her. "I don't need help," said Chelsea weakly.

"Too bad," said Kathy, laughing. "I'm going to help anyway. You'd do the same for me."

But she wouldn't! She couldn't because of her promise to Sidney.

"Well, let's go," said Kathy, tugging on Chelsea's arm. "Want me to carry the ads?"

Chelsea handed her half of what she had left, and they fell into step.

"Did you hear about the Sunday school picnic next week?" asked Kathy as they walked down Ash Street past Roxie's house toward the next home.

Chelsea shook her head. She'd been happy to learn Kathy went to the same church she did. It was scary to go to a Sunday school class full of strangers. Kathy had saved her a seat each week, and Chelsea had been very glad about that.

"It's at the park, and it's going to be an old-time picnic. We'll have races—even a three-legged race, and we'll churn our own ice cream and do lots of other fun things. Will you be my partner in the three-legged race?"

Chelsea desperately wanted to say yes, but she couldn't because of Sidney. "I don't know if I'll go," she said, walking faster.

"If you do go, will you be my partner?"

"I can't. I'm always Rob's partner at things like

127

that." That was true. Rob had always been too shy to find a partner for himself.

They reached the first house and had to stop talking about the picnic. Chelsea quickly told the woman who answered the door about the ad she held out to her. "Great or small, we do it all," she said, smiling.

"What a fine idea," said the woman as she scanned the ad. "I will keep you in mind." She smiled as she stepped back inside and closed her door.

At the next house Chelsea saw Gracie on the porch chewing on something. She raced up to the porch and shooed Gracie away.

Suddenly the door opened, and an old man stepped out, leaning heavily on a cane and scowling. "What d' you think you're doin' to my dog?" he said gruffly.

Chelsea flushed hotly. "I didn't know Gracie belonged to you. I'm sorry. I thought she was causing trouble again."

"My Gracie doesn't cause trouble! Now tell her you're sorry!" The man rapped his cane hard on the porch floor. "I won't have mean words said about Gracie!"

Chelsea wanted to turn and run, but Kathy stepped forward and quickly explained what they were doing.

"So you see we only wanted to help when we

saw the dog chewing on your slipper." Kathy pointed to the mangled footwear.

The man rubbed a big hand over his shallow cheek. "I can see where you'd get the idea she was doing wrong. I gave her that slipper last year when she first ruined it."

Chelsea started to walk away from the house, but Kathy stopped her and motioned to the ad in her hand. Reluctantly she handed the ad to the man. "Great or small, we do it all," she mumbled.

"I'll keep that in mind when I need somebody to tend Gracie," said the man, peering down at the ad.

Chelsea almost ran away from the house. She didn't want to hand out another ad. "I don't want to take care of Gracie," she said in a low, tight voice.

Kathy giggled. "You're the boss, Chelsea. You could give the job to Mike or Rob."

"That's right!" Chelsea giggled. "Or even Roxie!"

The next day Chelsea had already received two calls for lawn-mowing jobs. Since she was busy at Mrs. Sobol's, she assigned the work to Rob. He was thankful for it.

At Mrs. Sobol's Chelsea watched Mike laughing and talking with Mrs. Sobol as they weeded the flower gardens. They both laughed at the same things. They'd immediately loved each other, much to Chelsea's surprise.

Chelsea shook the last rug in the pile, then relaxed against the porch pillar. The first day Mike had come with her, he'd cleaned and swept the porch, making the house look much better.

With a tired sigh Chelsea carried the rugs back inside and put them in place. The house smelled like lemon spray. The phone rang, and Chelsea ran to answer it. Mrs. Sobol had asked her to answer it whenever she was busy or outdoors.

"Sobol residence," said Chelsea very efficiently. "Who's this?"

"Chelsea McCrea. I'm helping Mrs. Sobol. She's in the flower garden."

"Don't tell her I called."

"Who are you?"

"Don't matter."

"She'll want to know about this call." Chelsea gripped the receiver tightly. "Are you Pearl Phiffer?"

"No."

Chelsea searched for something to say. She felt the call was important, but she didn't know why. "Did you want to tell Mrs. Sobol something?"

"What kinda work have you done for her?"

"Cleaned the attic, packed things in boxes in the garage, and now I'm helping clean the rest of the house."

"What did she take from her attic?"

Chelsea leaned against the kitchen wall. "I don't know if I should tell."

"I'm part of the family. You can tell me."

Still Chelsea hesitated. "Are you Lissa?"

"No. Did you clean Lissa's room?"

"Yes. And Adam's."

"What about the room between theirs?"

Chelsea shook her head. "Mrs. Sobol always cleans that one herself. She wouldn't even let me touch the pink gingham rabbit that sits on the bed."

"Is the rabbit about three feet tall, and does it have plain pink floppy ears?"

"Yes." Chelsea heard a strange sound. "Are you crying?"

"What if I am?"

"Are you sure you don't want to talk to Mrs. Sobol?"

"No! How does she seem when she's in the bedroom with the pink rabbit?"

"Sad. I saw her sitting in the white rocking chair in there with the rabbit on her lap, and she rocked and prayed."

"Prayed?"

"For Penny."

"Are you sure?"

"Yes. I asked her about Penny, but she wouldn't answer me, so I didn't ask again." Chelsea chewed her bottom lip. "Are you Penny?"

"Yes."

Chelsea's stomach tightened. She'd seen a TV

show about a lost child. Was Penny Mrs. Sobol's lost child? "Are you coming home?"

"I don't know," said Penny in a weak voice.

"You should. Mrs. Sobol would like that. She is old, you know."

"Old?"

"And forgetful."

"I hadn't thought of that."

"Please let me call Mrs. Sobol so you can talk to her."

"I . . . can't . . . I . . . just . . . can't."

Chelsea searched her mind for more to say to keep Penny on the phone. Maybe Mrs. Sobol would come in and she could hand the phone to her. "Her sister Pearl is coming to live with her tomorrow. They were in a big fight."

"It was over me."

"I didn't know." Chelsea strained to see out the window. Mrs. Sobol and Mike were sitting in the grass laughing together. "You could come see her. And if you didn't want to stay, you could leave."

Penny was quiet a long time. "I could, couldn't I?"

"Yes. But Mrs. Sobol won't want you to leave. She'll want you to sleep in your bed. She keeps the sheets washed and the room spotless. She even sent the gingham rabbit to be dry-cleaned. But she made sure it was overnight service so it wouldn't be gone long."

Penny sobbed into the phone. "She always hated that rabbit. She said I was too old for it."

"She doesn't hate it now," said Chelsea.

"How old are you, Chelsea?"

"Eleven."

"I was sixteen when I left home."

"Oh." She was a runaway!

"I said I'd never return."

"You don't have to stay away just because you said that. God can help you and Mrs. Sobol be friends again." Chelsea twisted the cord around her finger. "You can come back anyway."

"Then I will!"

Chelsea gasped, and her heart leaped. "I'll tell Mrs. Sobol."

"No! Don't say a word! I mean it! I want to surprise her. I want to see her face so I know for sure she wants me."

"When will you come?"

"Tomorrow. I already have my plane ticket, but I wasn't sure if I'd use it."

"Do you need a ride from the airport?"

"Do you drive?" asked Penny.

Chelsea laughed. "No. But my mom or dad would pick you up. They like helping others."

"Aren't you going to ask me why I left home?"

"I guess. Why did you?"

Penny sighed. "Mom made me mad, and I said I'd never forgive her. I left and vowed to never stop

being angry at her. But now I can't remember what
she did that made me mad."

A band tightened around Chelsea's heart. She
said she'd never forgive Dad for making them move.
She knew she'd never run away from home. But she
had stopped having fun with Dad. She didn't talk to
him or play with him like she had before. "Did you
. . . forgive her?" asked Chelsea, suddenly feeling
close to tears.

"Yes. But by then I'd lost my nerve about coming home. You gave my courage back to me.
Thanks."

Chelsea laughed softly. She'd helped Penny! "I
wish you'd let me tell Mrs. Sobol."

"No. I want it this way. I'll probably see you
tomorrow. I'll find my own way to the house from
the airport. Thanks for offering to have your mom
or dad pick me up. I'd better go now. Bye, Chelsea.
Thanks again."

"Bye, Penny." Chelsea hung up the phone and
stood very still while the conversation ran over and
over in her mind.

13

Love

Chelsea scowled at Mike. He stood in the yard beside Mrs. Sobol looking as innocent as a baby. A robin flew down beside him, then flew away.

"Don't be angry with your sweet little brother, Chelsea," said Mrs. Sobol, patting Mike's blond head. "I asked him why you need to work, and he told me about your phone bill."

"I asked him not to tell," said Chelsea sharply.

"I forgot," said Mike with an innocent smile.

Chelsea could see an imp hiding behind the smile, but she didn't tell Mrs. Sobol. She'd never believe it anyway. "It's time to go home, Mike." She'd almost told Mrs. Sobol about Penny's call, but each time she opened her mouth, she snapped it closed. She'd promised not to tell. Unlike Mike, she'd keep her promise.

Mrs. Sobol folded her arms across her chest

and tilted her head. "Personally I feel your dad should pay the bill."

Chelsea's ears perked up. She liked what she'd just heard, especially coming from an adult.

"It was an honest mistake on your part," continued Mrs. Sobol.

"It was," said Chelsea. But inside she knew not *all* the phone calls had been honest mistakes. Maybe if she could get Dad to at least pay the "honest mistakes," she wouldn't have to work so long and hard to pay him back.

That evening Chelsea stood before Dad in his study. She'd given a lot of thought about asking him to pay the *whole* phone bill himself, and she'd come to the conclusion that she deserved to have him pay it. After all, he was the dad, and she was only a child. Why should she have to work to pay a bill? He was the dad. It was his job to pay bills, wasn't it?

"Whatever you want to say must be very important," said Dad with a chuckle. "Your cheeks are red as radishes."

"I've been thinking about the phone bill," she said in a clear, strong voice.

"Oh?" Dad walked around his desk and leaned back on it. He brushed a finger across his mustache and waited.

She locked her hands together behind her back

and didn't take her eyes off his. "I think you should pay the phone bill instead of me."

"And why is that?" he asked gently.

"Because I didn't realize I was doing anything wrong . . . And because you're the dad, and it's your job to pay the bills."

He pushed himself away from his desk and slipped his long arm around her shoulders. "Let's sit down and talk about this, shall we?"

She stiffened, but sat on the couch with him. She smelled his aftershave and felt the heat of his arm on her shoulders.

"Chelsea, I love you."

Right now she didn't believe that, but she didn't say so.

"And because I love you, I can't pay your phone bill."

She gasped and looked into his face. She couldn't believe it—he was serious!

"Honey, you have to learn to deal with the consequences of your actions. You made the calls. The consequence is the high phone bill. If I paid the bill for you, when something similar happened in the future you'd expect me to pay that too. And you'd never learn what you need to learn." He twisted a strand of her long red hair around his finger the way he'd done for as long as she could remember. "I want you to be the best person you can be. If you grew up expecting a handout all the time, you couldn't survive in this world. We're Christians, and we have God to help us, but even Christians must learn to follow some basic rules God has given us to live by."

Anger burned inside Chelsea, and she didn't want to sit and listen, but her hair was tangled around Dad's finger and she couldn't just jump up and run. Besides, he'd call her back until he was finished.

"It's up to your mom and me to teach you children how to live God's way. If I didn't care how you conducted yourself and if I didn't care if you learned anything, I'd pay the bill and be done with it. But I do care! I love you! Very, very much."

"But I need money!" she cried. "I can't even go shopping at the mall!"

"You'll have money as soon as you pay your phone bill. With all the work you'll get, it'll be paid before the end of the summer."

"The end of the summer?" She almost choked on the words. How could she survive that long? And what about the calls on next month's bill?

"It really isn't that long, honey. Time'll go fast since you'll be working every day." He tipped her chin up and looked into her face. "You'll feel very proud of yourself when you finally pay the bill. You'll know you did what you were supposed to do."

She wanted to yell at him and tell him just what

she thought of him and his ideas, but she knew he wouldn't take any sass. "I better go see if Rob took any more phone calls," she said just above a whisper. "Tomorrow I work for Mrs. Sobol, but I don't have anything after that."

"But you'll get something," said Dad with great assurance. "God is on your side! He wants you to overcome every obstacle."

Even dads? she thought to herself but not daring to ask the question aloud.

"You are to put on the whole armor of God so you are able to withstand all the fiery darts of Satan." Dad picked up Chelsea's hand from her lap and held it gently. "Honey, when you read and do God's Word, you're putting on His armor. When you obey and listen to me and your mom, you're maturing in the natural world. You have to grow spiritually, emotionally, and socially. I would be a terrible dad if I paid your phone bill for you. I love you, and I wish you hadn't made the bill, but you did, so we go from there."

Chelsea stared down at the gray carpet and longed to be in her room in Oklahoma by herself. "I wish we'd never moved," she said hoarsely.

"Honey, all the family has taken to our move. Rob actually has friends. Your mom has a new best friend, Kathy's mom. And Mike feels less like a baby. But you still walk around with a long face. You still wish you were back in Oklahoma."

"I never wanted to move," she whispered.

"I know. But we *did* move. You even have friends here already."

"Not a best friend!"

"You have friends who could turn into best friends. You have a whole heart full of love to give for a whole lot of friends. Don't narrow it down to one or two."

She bit her lip. He obviously didn't understand best friends at all!

"You have opportunities to work to make extra money once your bill is paid. And you like the church we go to. Let yourself like it here, hon bun."

Hon bun! He hadn't called her that in a long time. She softened a little, then hardened her heart. He was wrong! She couldn't like it here, and it wasn't fair for her to pay the phone bill.

He kissed both her cheeks. "I'm proud of you, hon bun."

She walked away without saying another word.

The next morning at Mrs. Sobol's house, Chelsea quickly finished the last bit of work. Mrs. Sobol paid her, but Chelsea kept hanging around. Every few minutes she glanced out the window. When was Penny coming? Had she changed her mind?

"Pearl won't be here until about 6, so stop looking for her," said Mrs. Sobol as she tested the chocolate cake in the oven. The aroma wafted through the kitchen.

"Smells good," said Chelsea. How could she keep her secret much longer?

"I wish Mike would've come," said Mrs. Sobol, taking the cake from the oven and setting it on a cooling rack. "I miss him."

"He had to help Mom," said Chelsea. She glanced out the window again, and her heart stopped. A car stood in the driveway, and a woman older than Mom was walking toward the front door. She was as tall as Mom, and her short, straight hair was brown. She wore beige slacks and a green blouse with beige trim. Was it Penny?

"Now what are you looking at?" asked Mrs. Sobol sharply. She stood beside Chelsea and peered out the window. "Who is that? Go see. If it's a saleslady, tell her I don't want any. I don't care what it is."

"Maybe you'd better answer," said Chelsea, trembling so badly she could barely stand up.

"Oh, all right! I didn't think you'd be so spineless!" Mrs. Sobol strode to the door.

Chelsea walked after her, her heart hammering loud enough for Kathy next door to hear.

Mrs. Sobol threw open the door, started to speak, but stopped. She clutched the door as the color drained from her face.

"Mom, it's me," whispered Penny.

"Penny! Oh, my dear Penny!" Mrs. Sobol burst into tears and drew Penny to her.

Chelsea blinked away tears and watched the two women hug each other. Finally they broke apart and stared at each other, then hugged again.

"I missed you so much," said Mrs. Sobol against Penny's head.

"I missed you," said Penny, pulling away slightly. "Forgive me for running away and for hurting you and Dad so much."

"I have." Mrs. Sobol pulled Penny inside and closed the door. "So did your dad."

"I'm glad," said Penny as fresh tears rolled down her face. Chelsea started for the door, then stopped to hear more. She wanted to make sure the reunion was just what Penny wanted.

"I thought you'd come for the funeral," said Mrs. Sobol.

"I did, but nobody saw me."

"Oh, I wish I would've seen you!" Mrs. Sobol wiped tears off her face with a tissue from her pocket. "Are you here to stay?"

"I have a family," said Penny. "So I can only stay a few days. But you could come back with me and meet them."

"A family! Do you have children?"

"Three. Rachel is fourteen, Phil eleven, and Marshall is nine."

"Marshall? After your dad." Mrs. Sobol

blinked as more tears ran down her face. "He'd have liked that."

Just then Penny noticed Chelsea. "You must be Chelsea."

"Yes." Chelsea smiled. She saw the surprise, then the questioning look on Mrs. Sobol's face.

Penny hugged Chelsea close. "Thanks again."

"What's this all about?" asked Mrs. Sobol sharply.

Penny laughed happily. "It's quite a story. Can we sit down before we fall down?"

"I've got to go home," Chelsea said. She slipped past them and rode her bike home. What a wonderful, happy ending to years of misery.

She thought about Dad as she parked her bike in the garage. Would she ever be able to run to him and hug him the way she once had? Would she even want to? What if she was an old woman and still angry at Dad?

"I wouldn't be mad if he'd just move us back home," she said grimly.

14

The Sunday School Picnic

Chelsea stood on the sidelines as the people gathered for the three-legged race. She'd planned to be Rob's partner just as she'd told Kathy, but he and Nick were partners, leaving Chelsea without one. The sun felt hot against her head. Smells of roasting chickens drifted out from the grill near the tables of food.

Dad stopped beside Chelsea. He wore jeans and a blue pullover shirt. His nose was red from being in the sun. "Would you like to race with me?" he asked with a chuckle.

"The three-legged race?" she asked in shock.

"Sure. I'm good at it. Want to give it a try?"

She didn't want to stand on the sidelines, so she nodded yes. She ran with Dad to the starting line. She'd worn jeans today just for the three-legged race. He tied their legs together, then whispered directions to her.

"We have to work as a team," he said. "We can't pull apart or we'll lose."

Chelsea nodded. Suddenly she laughed. It felt good to be in the race, especially when they had a chance to win because Dad knew how to run without tumbling over.

He bent down and kissed her cheek. "I love you, hon bun . . . even if we lose."

For right now she decided to forget her anger at him. She wanted to forget all the bad things she'd done since he'd first said they were going to move. "I love you too." Suddenly she realized she meant it. She *did* love him! She'd thought her love had died that day in Oklahoma.

She gripped the loop of Dad's jeans as they waited for the starting gun to go off. They had to run to the ribbon stretched between two tall maples. She glanced down the line of racers. Kathy was teamed with Hannah, Rob with Nick, and Roxie with a girl Chelsea didn't know. There were several people she'd seen in church, but she didn't remember their names. Could she and Dad really beat all the others?

The man in charge fired the gun. Chelsea jumped in surprise.

"Easy now," said Dad. "Start with our tied

legs, then run just as if you're running alone. Only keep ahold of my belt loop."

"I will." Chelsea did what Dad said, and they ran forward. Several couples were already sprawled on the ground, laughing and shouting. She and Dad had a late start, but they soon gained ground. She felt awkward tied to Dad, but they were running without falling. Most of the other racers tumbled over. Only Nick and Rob were ahead of them. Chelsea wanted to beat them, but they crossed the finish line just a few steps before she and Dad did.

"That was great, Chel!" Dad hugged her tight, then untied their legs.

She beamed with pride.

"You almost beat us," said Rob proudly.

"I know," said Chelsea, smiling at Rob. It no longer mattered that he was taking Nick's time.

"Want to look at the ducks with me, Chel?" asked Nick.

She looked at him in surprise. "Sure," she said, flushing.

"See you later, Rob," said Nick.

"Thanks for the race, Chel," said Dad, smiling down at her.

"It was fun," she said, and she really meant it. She walked to the river with Nick while he talked about the race. They stopped at the edge of the water and watched the ducks diving after the bread people were tossing in.

"Look at that duck," said Nick, pointing to a black duck diving for a potato chip someone had tossed in the water. "Rob and I were here a while ago feeding the ducks. I wanted to save some bread for you, but I ran out."

"That's all right," said Chelsea. It made her feel good that he'd even thought about her.

They walked along the edge of the water and talked about school and about *King's Kids*. She looked around for Kathy and found her with Hannah watching a game of horseshoe. She liked being with Nick, but she suddenly realized she liked being with the girls even better. It was easier to talk to them than to Nick.

"I joined the computer club at school," said Nick. "I told Rob about it and he's going to join too. Would you like to?"

"I don't know enough about computers," said Chelsea. It sounded boring to her.

Just then over the quack of the ducks she heard her mom's laughter. Chelsea glanced around and saw Mom talking and laughing with Grace Aber. Chelsea hadn't seen Mom laugh like that since they'd left Oklahoma. Dad had said Mom had found a new best friend, but Chelsea hadn't believed him. Maybe it was true.

Several minutes later Nick ran to join Rob, and Chelsea started walking toward Hannah and Kathy. Dad stood alone near a trash barrel between her and the girls. A wave of love for Dad rose inside Chelsea and washed over her. She wanted to tell him she was sorry for being angry and even sorry for disobeying him. She didn't want to wait until they got home. It seemed important to tell him right now.

She stopped beside him and said, "Hi."

He winked at her. "Nice picnic, isn't it?"

She nodded.

"I can tell you have something on your mind," he said, tugging her red ponytail. "I've been praying for you, hon bun."

Tears blurred her vision as she caught his hand and gripped it between both of hers. "I'm sorry for being mad at you for making us move," she said.

"I forgive you," he said softly.

"There's more."

"Oh?" He cocked his brow.

"I . . . I . . . called Sid again . . . after you said not to."

"I know," he said tenderly. "I've been waiting for you to tell me."

She threw her arms around him and clung to him as she told him about the call and how sorry she was. "I promise to pay for it," she said.

"I know," he said. "I am so glad to have my girl back! I've missed you!"

"I've missed you too," she said with a catch in her voice.

He wiped tears off her freckled cheeks with his

thumbs. "You've asked me to forgive you. Now ask Jesus to forgive you also. He's ready and willing even more than I was. He loves you, Chelsea. He wants to help you, but He can't if you don't let Him. He'll help you get used to living here. He'll help you find friends. And He'll help you obey."

"I know," she whispered. She closed her eyes and leaned her forehead against Dad's chest. "I'm sorry, Jesus. Forgive me for disobeying and for being angry. I love You, and I want to be like You."

"Now you're free, Chel. Instead of letting Jesus help you all this time, you refused to go to Him. That always makes life harder. Jesus is your Best Friend and your very own Savior. But He can't force Himself on you. Never turn away from Him when you're hurting or angry. Turn to Him for help."

"I will," she said, sniffing back tears. "I promise." And she meant it.

"Your mom and I have been praying for you. And God always answers prayer. Always!"

"I'm glad," Chelsea said.

Dad kissed her cheek. "Go have fun now, hon bun. And don't be afraid to let Hannah and Kathy be friends with you."

She ran toward Hannah and Kathy. She could do things together with the girls, but they would never be her best friend. Sid was her best friend forever! That's just the way it was.

Best Friends

Chelsea fingered the *I'm A Best Friend* button she'd pinned to her T-shirt to remind her to keep her distance from Hannah and Kathy as they talked about *King's Kids*. Kathy's dad had agreed to let Kathy add her name to the list and take jobs when she could. Two weeks had gone by since they'd handed out the ads, and several people had called already. Most of the work was yardwork, sometimes it was baby-sitting, and sometimes it was doing light housecleaning, but no one cared what tasks they got. They were all just glad to get paid.

From where she sat in the living room Chelsea heard the familiar clink of the mailbox lid. She hurried to the door and pulled the stack of mail out. Would there be a phone bill? How glad she was she'd told Dad about her last call! She leaned against the closed door and looked through the stack. She found a letter addressed to her. "It's from

Sid!" Her heart leaped with joy at seeing Sid's handwriting.

Chelsea finished looking through the pile, carried the mail to Dad's study, then ran to her room to read her letter. If Hannah and Kathy came, they'd have to wait for her.

She touched Sid's picture and smiled. She tore open the envelope and rubbed her hand over Sid's familiar scrawl, then read:

Dear Chel,

It is 110 out today. I bet you're glad you're in Michigan. I wish I was there with you. I know there's no snow now, but I bet it's not really really hot like here.

I guess I better tell you why I'm writing. I don't want to hurt your feelings, but Megan Richfield is my new best friend. We settled our fight and decided to be best friends from now on. We are going to start a King's Kid business here just like yours. Megan will be the boss. We will even use your slogan: "Great or small, we do it all!" It's a good slogan. I hope nobody asks me to take a tick out of their dog's ear. That would make me very sick.

I hope you are having fun with your new friends Hannah and Kathy.

Love always,
Sidney Boyer

Chelsea leaned weakly back in her chair. All of her tears seemed dried up. Now she had no best friend! Slowly she unpinned her button and dropped it on the desk. She turned Sidney's picture over, then reread the letter. She dropped it as if it were a burning match that scorched her fingers.

Just then Roxie Shoulders walked into the bedroom. "Rob said you were up here," said Roxie.

Chelsea stared blankly at her.

Roxie dropped on her knees beside Chelsea's chair. "Is something wrong? Should I call your mom?"

"I don't have a best friend any longer," said Chelsea woodenly.

Roxie picked up Sid's letter and read through it quickly. "I'm sorry, Chel . . . Really sorry. I wish I could say something to make you feel better."

Before Chelsea could answer, Hannah and Kathy walked into the bedroom. They looked ready to burst with excitement.

"Your mom said to come right up," said Hannah, her dark eyes sparkling.

"What's wrong, Chelsea?" asked Kathy, frowning slightly.

"Her best friend broke up with her," said Roxie sharply. "I can't believe anyone would be so mean!"

Tears filled Chelsea's eyes and slipped down her cheeks. "I want to be alone," she whispered as she stood.

"No way!" cried Roxie. "This is not the time to be alone, is it, girls?"

"No," Hannah and Kathy said together.

"We're going to cheer you up," said Kathy with a small laugh.

"Jesus loves you," said Hannah. "And we do too."

"That's right," said Kathy.

"I can learn to love you," said Roxie. "You did help me, and you did add my name to the list of *King's Kids*."

Suddenly Chelsea didn't hate Roxie any more. She could see the kindness in her that Rob had seen.

"You have a Friend who sticks closer than a brother or sister or even a best friend," said Hannah.

"It's Jesus," Kathy and Roxie said at the same time.

"I know," whispered Chelsea as she sank to the edge of her bed. Hannah sat on one side of her and Roxie the other. Kathy sat on the floor at her feet. Chelsea looked from one girl to the other. Sid had always been her best friend. How could she suddenly not have Sid as a best friend?

"I think we should have a *King's Kid* meeting to get your mind off your problems," said Hannah.

"I agree," said Kathy.

"Me too," said Roxie. "But if you want to talk about how you feel, you can. It helps sometimes."

Chelsea sniffed and rubbed her hand over her nose. "You should all go home and leave me alone."

Roxie tapped Chelsea on the shoulder. "We already agreed we wouldn't do that. So get used to us being here."

Hannah laughed. "We could tell jokes if you want."

"I could stand on my head," said Kathy. "Not as good as Mike can, though."

"Let's just have our meeting," said Roxie sharply. "We don't have to act stupid." She tapped Chelsea again. "You're the president. Call the meeting to order."

Chelsea took a deep breath and called the meeting to order. "Rob says we should elect a secretary, a treasurer, and a vice president to take over when I can't conduct the meeting." She almost choked on her words, but forced herself to continue. She wouldn't think about Sid. They'd have their meeting, then go on from there.

"There are four of us," said Hannah, "and four offices. We could each hold an office."

"Good idea," said Chelsea. "Who can write the best?"

"Not me," said Roxie.

"Get a paper and everyone write a sentence,"

said Chelsea. "Whoever writes the clearest will be the secretary."

"I can make change," said Hannah. "I'd make a good treasurer."

"Write your sentence," Roxie said impatiently as she handed Hannah the notebook Chelsea had found. "And don't try to be sloppy on purpose."

Chelsea watched as they each wrote a sentence. Roxie had the neatest handwriting, so she was chosen as secretary.

"I can't believe my handwriting is the best," said Roxie, studying it again.

"You'll keep notes of each meeting," said Chelsea. "So start with this one."

"List the times that each *King's Kid* can work," said Hannah. "Yesterday I couldn't take the job given to me because it was the wrong time."

"How're we going to handle the money?" asked Kathy.

"Who's going to handle the money?" asked Hannah.

"You can," said Chelsea. "Is that all right with the rest of you?"

"Sure," they said.

"What money will I handle?" asked Hannah.

"This is a business," said Chelsea, trying to think just what she was going to say. "I say instead of this being my business, it'll be all of ours—all the *King's Kids*."

"Great idea!" cried Roxie. "I'd work harder if I knew it was my business too."

"We all have to do our very best work or we can't be in the group," said Hannah. "Don't you think so, Chel?"

"Yes. We have to do good work so we'll get called again." Chelsea got so involved with the meeting that she forgot all about the agony she'd felt from Sid's letter.

"Guess what, everybody?" Kathy looked around the group. "That leaves me as vice president," she said with a happy laugh. "So what do *I* do?"

"Take over when I'm gone," said Chelsea.

"When will that be?" asked Kathy.

Chelsea shrugged, then laughed. "Never, I guess. But we'll give you something to do. I just can't think of it right now."

"You could find a way to make Gracie stay home," said Roxie. "I couldn't get what Rob suggested because it cost too much. She started digging in the flowers again. And Mom is determined to win the Prettiest Flowers Contest this year."

"She won last year, didn't she?" asked Hannah.

Roxie nodded. "She wants to win every year. But she can't if we don't do something about Gracie."

"How about asking her owner to keep her

home?" said Chelsea. "Kathy and I met him the other day."

"Ezra Menski's his name," said Roxie. "And he hates me because I always complain about Gracie."

"Kathy, do you want the job of talking to him?" asked Chelsea.

"I guess I could talk to him," said Kathy, wrinkling her nose. "I'm getting a lot of practice talking to old people by talking to Mrs. Sobol and her sister."

"I've written it down, so you have to," said Roxie, lifting her pencil high.

"I think we should vote on how many can be in the business," said Chelsea. "We can't handle every person in the world who wants to."

"I have a superb idea!" cried Hannah, jumping up. "Just wait'll you hear!"

"Tell us," said Roxie, her pencil poised.

"We should have only ten people to a group. But we can have lots of groups! If, say, Linda Hanover from Beechnut Street wants to be in our group and we already have ten, we tell her to start her own group. We give them the rules to follow, and they each have officers. If we get too many jobs, we'll hand them over to another group. How does that sound?"

"I like it," said Kathy.

"Me too," said Chelsea and Roxie.

"And nobody can go from group to group,"

said Chelsea. "If your name is on one group, you stay with them . . . unless you have an extra-good reason for switching." She looked at Roxie's paper. "Did you get that down?"

"Yes." Roxie wrote for a long time, then lifted her head. "Anything else?"

"What about dues?" asked Hannah. "Don't we need to have dues?"

"Not exactly dues," said Chelsea. She remembered paying dues in the girls' club she was in. "Since this is a business we should take a small percent of what each one makes. It'll cover the cost of printing ads and other things we can't think of right now."

They all agreed, then Chelsea waited for Roxie to write it down. Already she'd filled three pages. But then, she wrote big.

"Anything else?" asked Chelsea. She was really enjoying herself.

Hannah raised her hand.

"What?" asked Chelsea.

Hannah stood up and folded her hands in front of her. "I say we do at least three good deeds a week. If we see that someone can't really pay for work, we do it for free just to help them out."

"That's crazy," said Roxie.

"I vote yes," said Kathy.

"Me too," said Chelsea.

Roxie frowned. "Oh, all right. I guess it

wouldn't hurt me to do a good deed . . . as long as it's not too often."

"This meeting is getting to be too long," said Chelsea, glancing at her clock. "I say we quit and meet again next week. We'll meet once a week and see if everything's going right."

"I agree!" said Roxie, Hannah, and Kathy at the same time. Then they burst out laughing.

"Let's go downstairs and see if we can bake cookies," said Chelsea, leading the way. "Chocolate-chip cookies with M & Ms."

"And nuts," said Kathy.

"Not nuts," said Hannah. "I don't like nuts."

Chelsea stopped in the kitchen, and the girls swarmed around her, laughing and talking. It felt good to have them there. They were her friends! Maybe someday they'd be her best friends. She laughed as she pulled out the big mixing bowl.

You are invited to become a
Best Friends Member!

In becoming a member you'll receive a club membership
card with your name on the front and a list of the Best
Friends and their favorite Bible verses on the back along
with a space for your favorite Scripture. You'll also receive
a colorful, 2-inch, specially-made I'M A BEST FRIEND button and a write-up about the author, Hilda Stahl, with her
autograph. As a bonus you'll get an occasional newsletter
about the upcoming BEST FRIENDS books.

All you need to do is mail your NAME, ADDRESS (printed
neatly, please), AGE and $3.00 for postage and handling to:

BEST FRIENDS
P.O. Box 96
Freeport, MI 49325

WELCOME TO THE CLUB!

(Authorized by the author, Hilda Stahl)